Cops Murdered My Brother so

What do I do now?

By

Jorge Martinez

Dedicated to my brother

Alejandro Perez Martinez

I do not know where you are at right now, but I will find you soon. I want you to understand to never give up on where ever you are at right now and to remember I will find you. No matter what happens in your future and in my future, I will make sure that you get your justice at any cost. I love you in this world and in the next world.

ISBN: 978-0-578-10065-4

Dear reader,

You have no clue if this story of my brother's life and my life is going to be true or not because the police are telling lies to cover up my brother's murder! I am going to change people's names, dates, areas where I lived, etc, in this book because it will be a fictional book for legal reasons. The reason I am saying this book is going to be fictional is because some chapters of the book will explain what I wanted to do to these corrupted cops and the people who covered up his murder! However, please after reading this book and after telling your family members and friends about this book, please don't harm any cop or anybody associated with the government.

I want to live a private life because after people read this book, everyone is going to be amazed on how much power I have and the things I know. Also I don't like how Hollywood treats people and I don't want the media to follow me around. I just want to tell the truth on how my brother was executed so you can understand the TRUTH and not the fucking lies that the police are trying to cover up! I want to live a normal life and I want my family, friends, and Alex to not be bothered by the media so after you read this book, please respect our privacy and hopefully you question on what the police have said about this case.

This is going to be a story about my past, present life, and future life? You will read a lot of repetitive information because my mind can't stop remembering the things that happened to my brother and me. I also tend to jump from one subject to another subject because my mind starts to remember all my emotions that occurred through the day my brother was murdered and all the great times I spent with him. I hardly ever swear in life so if I do start to swear in this book, you will understand that I am very angry and I want to prove my point. However, I hardly swear so you will hardly read any outrages words.

Please understand that I never wanted to write a book about my brother's tragedy, but I do want people to know the truth on what happened to my brother. I saw my brother brutally murdered by these fucking corrupted cops and I can't stop my mind seeing my brother keep getting shot when he was on the fucking ground! So one day I just started writing and I didn't stop writing until I wrote the entire truth. I have never been so angry in my life so my family members, friends, and my psychiatrist told me that I needed to let go all of my emotions and everything that happened to me before it destroys my mind. It was really hard to write about this horrible tragedy, but I know in the end, people will realize the truth and the cops can't stop me from writing the truth. (The pen is mightier than the sword) Also I need to let you know, I use to be someone that could do anything in life, but right now I can't even look at myself in the mirror.

To all the men and woman who read this book, here is a quick message: We are all created equal and have a choice to live a certain way. My brother wasn't perfect growing up and I wasn't perfect growing up. However, we did try our best to live a good life, but things changed and now I am going to do anything that is possible to make sure these cops and all the people who are trying to cover it up.... Get caught on their lies and be punished by the court system or I will do something about it. Trust me, you don't want me to do my own justice because there will be plenty of consequences and plenty of people who will never live the same way again. Also remember I use to be a "Good" person in this world, but once you have seen what I saw on February 28th 2011 in Lynden Washington when my brother was brutally murdered, I died, and I became a different person.

I hope after you read this book on why I had to do what I needed to do, you get to understand the truth and how much pain I am in. My goal isn't for you to feel sorry for me, but at the end of this book I will explain my goal to you so you can understand what one little thing in life can change everyone's life as well.

I am not selling this book to make money. 50% of the money goes to taxes and the publisher. The other 40% will go to Alex's daughter, family members, friends, and charities. The remaining 10% will go to my medical bills. I don't need the money to survive, I just want to get justice.

The Truth

The month before February 28th 2011, my brother Alex and I were playing basketball near where we lived. He was telling me that he wanted to move to a new house or into an apartment, but I told him if we stayed at our current place then in another year I would have enough money to buy a house and buy the business near where we lived. He agreed and we went back home to watch television. My brother would usually stay home all day to either sleep or watch television. I would work full time and when I got home, I would take care of my brother by taking him to the store or he would take the car to drive around and just listen to music.

One day after we went to the store to buy groceries, my brother came out of his room a little upset because he thought someone was in his room. Nobody went into his room, but since my brother was hit with a baseball bat in the head over thirteen years ago, he wasn't mentally himself anymore. I tried to convince my brother to go to the hospital so he can get some new medicine, but he told me that he was a little tired at the moment and wanted to sleep. When my brother woke up, he started to break some stuff in his room and in the bathroom. I went into his room and asked him why he was breaking things and he told me that he wanted me to change things in the house so things would be newer and better. So I agreed and I told him that I would upgrade things, but that he needed to go to the hospital to get new medicine. He agreed, and that's when I got information to contact a psychiatrist for the mentally ill.

After talking to a psychiatrist, I went down to her office to write down what my brother symptoms were. They told me that it would be best to have an officer come down to the house so they can take him to the hospital so they can evaluate him. So when the police were contacted, I met them outside to tell them the situation and they walked inside the house with me into my brother's room. They asked my brother to get up and turn around so they could handcuff him to take him to the hospital. My brother complied and he was taken to the hospital for some evaluations. I talked to my brother that night and he told me he was happy he was in the hospital to get some new medicine.

Alex spent 15 days at the hospital so they could evaluate him again and they gave him some new medicine. I would go hang out with him at the hospital on some nights after work and we would just watch television and talk about what he wants. After those 15 days, I picked him up and his doctor told me that he would go see a counselor once a week and that I had to take him to see his doctor too so he could get his medicine once a month. Once we got home that night, I showed my brother that I got a new car so that way he could drive to the store or wherever he wanted to go when I was working. He was very happy again and things seemed like everything was normal again. However, since my brother got hit in the head with a baseball bat a long time ago, he tends to forget some things from time to time, but whenever I am around him he calms down and he trust me to take care of him. So.........

On February 28th 2011, everything changed. I was at the gym that morning when my dad called me and asked me if I took Alex back to the hospital, but I told him that I didn't take him. So he told me that he called the police because he couldn't find Alex and that he was breaking some things at the house again. So I took off to the house right away and got there within five minutes. My dad was outside looking for Alex because he didn't find him inside the house. So I parked the car where my dad was standing and walked inside the house.

When I walked into the house, I saw a lot of stuff was broken again and Alex was sitting on the couch. I sat down right next to my brother and I asked Alex why he broke everything again and he told me, "George, I don't want you to fix the house anymore and I rather us live in a new house or at an apartment." So I told him that he was right, but my dad already called the cops and they are already on their way. I also called his counselor and he told me that he would meet Alex at the hospital so he could talk to him. So I asked Alex, "Do you want me to take you to the hospital?" Alex said, "No, I want the police to take me to the hospital and I want you to find a house or an apartment so you can show me at the hospital tonight on where we will live." So I grabbed his jacket out of his room and I told Alex that I am going to step outside to talk to the police and tell them that you are ready to go to the hospital. So Alex said, "I am sorry I broke everything, but I knew if I broke everything than you couldn't fix everything and that you had to find a new place to live." So I told Alex that I understood and that everything would be OK.

When I stepped outside, I noticed the police were still not there so I called 911 to find out where they were at and I was even thinking to stop them from coming to the house because I was going to take my brother to the hospital. When the dispatcher answered, I noticed the police were coming so I said a few words then hanged up and approached the police to tell them the situation. There was four police officers that came to the house, I told them that my brother was mentally ill because he was hit in the head with a baseball bat a long time ago, but that I just talked to him and he is ready to go to the hospital. They asked me if we had any guns or knives in our house, but I told them that we don't and all we have is kitchen knives. So all four police officers started walking towards the house with my dad and me. Three of the officers entered the garage with my dad, but the fourth officer told me that I couldn't enter the garage because the cops would take care of the situation. So I started to walk behind my dad's truck so I could enter the garage where the officer wasn't standing.

When I was about to enter the garage, I saw and heard officer #3 yell, "Alex come out of the house." Alex walked out of the house and saw four police officers, my dad, and I waiting for him to come out. When he was coming out of the house to enter the garage, he was looking at the officers' kind of surprise because he didn't understand why there were so many police officers at the house. When Alex was walking into the garage, he kept his eyes at the police, then me, and then he missed one of the steps and stumbled on the steps of the stairs entering the garage. While Alex was going to fall down officer #3 went towards him to catch him from falling and when the officer and my brother collided, the flashlight my brother had fell and hit the side of the house (you could hear a loud "bang" when the flashlight hit the side of the house) and then both the officer and my brother fell down on ground. The officer #3 fell back and hit his head against a wooden box and a big tool box. Then while my brother Alex was about to stand up with nothing in his hands, officer #2 shot my brother while only being four feet away from him. My brother fell onto the ground right away again and the second shot that officer

#2 shot, hit the house. Then officer #2 shot four more shots when my brother was on the ground. Then officer #1 started shooting my brother seven times when my brother was still on the ground.

The entire time Alex was on the ground, I thought the officers were shooting bean bags or rubber bullets because I didn't think they would be shooting a human being on the ground. After all the shots were fired, my dad turned around because he was standing in between both officers when they were shooting Alex on the ground so once I saw my dad walk out of the garage with an angry look on his face, that's when I started to walk around my dad's truck to meet my dad leaving the garage. However, officer #4 started walking towards me and grabbed me so he wouldn't let me enter the garage and that is when I knew something was wrong. So I pushed officer #4 away from me and ran towards my brother on the ground. Alex stomach was still moving, but his mouth wasn't moving that much. I noticed all the bullet shots on my brother so I started to give my brother CPR. Officer #1 was to my left on the ground looking for something, but the only thing he found was a flashlight. Officer #2 was still standing to my right while I was giving my brother CPR. Then after a few moments of giving my brother CPR, my brother was trying to breathe out of his mouth and then he barely started to say a few words out of his mouth, but then officer #1 used his shoulder to tackle me off my brother. He then rolled my brother over onto his stomach to handcuff him. I then said, "Why the fuck are you handcuffing him, you just shot him like 12 times!" So then I said, "He needs CPR, you need to give him CPR, please give him CPR!"

I then turned around and said to officer #2, "Why did

you shoot him?" and officer #2 said, "I thought he had a hammer?" so I said, "What fucking hammer, show me a fucking hammer, there wasn't a hammer?" Officer #1 had the flashlight in his hand and said, "I thought I heard a gun shot?" Then I hear behind me, "Officer down, gun shots fired, officer down." So then they asked the officer #3 if he was ok and he kept on saying, "I am ok, I am ok." And that he hit his head against something when he fell down. So I kept on yelling at the cops to give my brother CPR because he was on his stomach and I noticed he stopped breathing again! But Officer #4 and Officer #2 kept on pushing me out of the garage! However, I wouldn't leave the garage so they had to drag me out of the garage! So I kept on saying, "My brother needs CPR! He needs help! Why don't you give him CPR? If you don't want to give him CPR, why don't you let me give him CPR?" (My brother was on his stomach hand cuffed and he wasn't moving anymore!)

When I was standing outside the garage looking inside, my dad kept on asking the officers, "You guys are so stupid why did you shoot him, please tell me why did you shoot him?" And both officers were just looking at each other and didn't know what to say. So I kept on yelling at the cops that my brother needs CPR, but then officer #1 dragged my brother's body away and towards the house door. Officer #2 started moving things around in the garage to make more room for officer #3 to lie down and to help the bleeding stop where he landed from. I kept on looking inside the garage and my head was like I was going in circles because I didn't know what to do. So after a few minutes standing outside of the garage, I then decided to call 911 so I could report that these cops don't know what they are doing and we need someone to give CPR to my brother! I grabbed my cell phone from my shorts and when I was pushing 911 on my cell phone, that's when two border agents with two assault rifles started running towards the house. Officer #5 and Officer #6 started yelling at me, "Throw down your gun, throw down your gun!" so I looked behind me because I didn't think they were talking to me.

The officers kept on yelling at me again, "Throw down your gun!" So I yelled back to them, "I don't have a gun, this is my cell phone." But again the officers kept on yelling, "Throw down your gun!" And then Officer #5 said, "Last warning!" and then he put his eye onto his scope of his assault rifle so that is when I said, "Holy shit!" And I jumped onto the ground underneath my dad's truck and then I threw my cell phone towards the cops. Then officer #4 and my dad ran out of the garage waving their hands and officer #4 said, "No, no, no, this is his brother!" so officer #5 and officer # 6 ran towards the garage and asked, "Where's the gun?" And I said, "I didn't have a gun, I had my cell phone! And my brother needs CPR!" But officer #5 wanted to search us so my dad and I were put on the ground so they could search us for weapons. After they searched us and found nothing on us, they kept on pushing us away from the garage. Officer #1, 2, 3 were still in the garage this entire time!

If you are wondering why my brother had a flashlight, well he is mentally ill and like every day he always carries something on him. He usually he carries his pack of cigarettes or his iPod, but at night he always carries his flashlight when he goes outside to have a smoke. Since he was breaking a lot of the windows and other stuff inside the house with the flashlight, he came outside when the police told him to come outside. I am assuming he came outside with the flashlight to give to my dad or to the police because he was breaking a lot of things with the flashlight. (The flashlight is the kind of flashlight that police officer's use.) He didn't have a hammer and he only had a flashlight!

Who searches the brother and the father after a human being was shot at 13 times? Why didn't they give my brother CPR during this time? Officer #6 grabbed a chair and told us to sit down so my dad sat down away from the garage. We couldn't see in the garage anymore so I kept on trying to walk into the garage, but the cops wouldn't let me in or near the garage anymore. Then I over heard one of the cops say, "Why did you handcuff him?" And then you could see the cops were trying to move things around again like the tool boxes, my brother's body, and all the little things that were in the garage. I kept on telling the officers around me that my brother needs CPR, but they were ignoring what I had to say. Then more and more officers were coming onto the scene, while officer #1, 2, and 3 were still in the garage!

I tried calling my sister, but she didn't pick up her phone. So I called my uncle and told him that the cops just killed Alex. He wanted to know why, but I said, "I don't know why?" But I was trying to get a hold of my sister so they tried calling her too! So while I was trying to call my sister again... A new officer who wasn't wearing a uniform started talking to my dad. He asked him, "What happened here?" And my dad said, "Those cops are stupid, those cops are stupid because my son had a flashlight! They kept on shooting my son and I don't know why?" So I told my dad to stop talking to the cops because first, I was scared they might shoot at us again. Second, every time I kept on telling them that my brother needed CPR, they weren't helping Alex. Third, if we say one thing, they will repeat it to the news or in court and trust me, I wasn't going to say what I wanted to say because this is what I was going to say after I saw my brother brutally murdered when he was on the ground!!!

"You fucking stupid motherfucking cops just killed my brother for no reason and I am going to kill them and anyone who stands in my way! You have no fucking clue what you just did, but I am going to make sure you fucking die!!! You guys have no clue who I am and just wait until I get out of here; I am going to kill everyone and anyone who stands in my way!!!"

I finally got a hold of my sister and she was crying. She wanted to know why the cops killed Alex and I said, "I don't know why?" Everything happened so fast and he was lying on the ground." We both hanged up and the cops kept on asking my dad why the cops shot Alex. So I said, "Don't they teach you guys ethics in cops training school? If you just saw your son or your brother keep getting shot when he was on the ground, wouldn't you want respect and be left alone?" So one of the officers said, "We didn't get trained on any ethics class." So I told them, "Well obviously you guys don't know how to do your job!" By this time two ambulances came to our house and officer #1, 2, and 3 were still in the garage! (These cops were in the garage for over an hour!) Some officers brought Alex's body out of the garage and put him on the ground. Some medics put something on my brother's mouth and then checked his eyes. I asked one of the officers, "Aren't you guys going to give my brother CPR now?" And he said, "No, because he is dead and now this is a homicide." And that's when my mind started to go numb............

I couldn't think straight anymore, I could hear people

talking, but I really didn't know much what they were saying. I wanted to get out of there, but my dad didn't want to leave. He kept on asking different officers on why they shot his son, but nobody could explain to him why? I seriously wanted to get out of there because nothing made sense! It seemed like everything was a horrible nightmare or if I was in a horrible coma! It didn't seem like I was alive and it seemed like I was in HELL. So I finally convinced myself to leave and I kept on begging my dad to leave with me, but he didn't want to leave. He told me that I should leave and to come back an a hour to pick him up. Then I saw officer #3 getting taken out in a stretcher and his head was wrapped up. He had some blood spots on his head because he fell on something hard, but he was fine and officer #2 was standing right next to him smiling. I still remember his smile because it seemed like he was laughing coming out of the garage!

So that is when I left.......

When I finally got out of there, my dad stayed behind because he still wanted to know why the cops shot his son. The entire street was closed down and there was over 100 cops at our house or near our house. Once I left the house, I drove around, and then pulled over to puke. I kept on telling myself that this wasn't real and that everything was a horrible nightmare. I kept on trying to wake up by yelling as loud as I can in my car, but I couldn't wake up so I kept on yelling. I kept on telling myself that nothing made sense so this all had to be a horrible dream! So I drove around for a half hour and then I tried to go back home to pick up my dad.

The road was closed so I tried calling my dad so I could pick him up. However, the police kept on questioning him, but I kept on yelling at him because I didn't feel he was safe being there. The police wouldn't let me back to the house so I had to keep on calling my dad on his cell phone. Even one officer took his cell phone from him and he said, "Jesus (Jesus is my dad's name) can't talk right now because he has to talk to us." And I told the officer that he doesn't have to talk to anyone because he didn't do anything wrong!" So he hanged up and I kept on calling my dad, but my dad kept on coming on the phone for a second, but then he would hang up. He finally started to leave the house after 15 minutes of me calling him.

We started to drive around and then I went to a gas station to pick up a pack of smokes and a can of beer because my hand was shaking. My dad has never seen me drink and he has never seen me smoke. However, I needed something to calm me down because my dad kept on praying. My dad is a really religious person so he prays every day, he reads the bible every day, and he goes to church at least once a week. He was praying while we were in the car, but I just kept on drinking and smoking. He told me that I shouldn't drink and smoke, but I told him if I didn't smoke or drink then I was going to go get a gun and shoot every fucking cop at our house! He kept on telling me that violence is never the answer and that we need to be strong and to tell the truth. But I told him that things won't be OK and these cops are probably going to kill us to keep our mouths shut, but he kept on praying and said, "Don't worry these cops will tell the truth and they will go to jail." And that's when I said, "If these cops don't go to jail then I am going to kill these cops!" So my dad kept on praying to God to calm me down and to look over Alex.

After driving around for two hours, my sister called me

and said, "Why are the cops saying Alex was trying to hit an officer with a hammer?" And I said, "What are you talking about? That was bullshit, the only thing Alex had was a flashlight!" So I told my dad what my sister just told me and that's when he got all mad and said that was a bunch of lies. So we got a hold of the local news and we told them our side of the story. They told us that Alex was running out of the house swinging a hammer and I was so amazed on what they were saying because NOTHING they said was true. (Also a person who I met after all this happened, told me he was listening to the police scanner that day, and he heard on the police scanner, "A male ran out the house and tried to attack an officer with a hammer.") So then I started to get calls from different news channels and they wanted to know our side of the story. So then I did a TV interview and explained what I saw and everything I am hearing from different people didn't make sense?

I guess first they reported that Alex ran out of the house swinging a hammer which was false. Then they said that one of the officers tried to taser Alex, but that was false. Then they said that they had no choice, but to shoot Alex. However, they didn't want to say how many times they shot him. I told them that I knew that the cops shot him at least six times because they kept on shooting my brother when he was on the ground! After the first shot, Alex started to fall on the ground and that's when both officers started to shoot Alex multiple times, but I couldn't count all the shots because everything happened so fast. And they just kept on shooting him when he was on the ground and I kept on thinking that they were shooting rubber bullets or bean bags because I never thought police officers would shoot someone when they are on the ground only three or four feet away from them.

My dad and I went to my uncle's house that night because the police were still investigating our house. They told my dad we couldn't go back home until their investigation was over. That night we just started to drink pretty much all night because nothing made sense. We even watched the Sheriff go on television and explain their side of their story. They first said there was only three officers on scene, but there was FOUR police officers on scene. They were explaining all their lies and that my brother had a bad criminal history. He kept on telling how my brother was a bad criminal and that he was trying to kill an officer with a hammer. I was in a complete shock because nothing he was saying is what happened?

Do you know how your mind feels like when you see or hear someone tell a story that was complete bullshit? That is why the entire day and the entire night felt like nothing was real and it felt like I was in HELL. Because even after everything I saw that day, they were telling a complete different story on television! My dad got a call from the police that night and they told us that we still couldn't go back to the house and that we could probably go back to the house the next day. So that entire night, I was calling family members and friends to tell them what happened. A lot of people were angry because everything that they saw on television didn't make sense and they didn't know how many times Alex was shot. Also a lot of people were mad because they didn't know that the police tackled me off Alex when I was giving him CPR and then they rolled him over and handcuffed him. Who the fuck rolls a person over and handcuffs them after they shoot at a person 13 times?

The next day when we got to the house, the entire garage was taken apart. It seems like the police took everything out of my dad's garage and they were searching for something? We think they were searching for some guns or knives because they couldn't find a gun on me or on Alex. One of the officer's thought Alex might have had a gun on him too so that is why they searched the entire garage and inside the house. They couldn't find a gun or knife because my dad doesn't own any kind of weapon except a kitchen knife. But seriously our entire garage was taken apart and everything was moved around. There was a lot of blood on the ground and there was still a lot of blood where my brother was on the ground and where his body was dragged towards the house door. I still don't know why the cop was dragging my brother's body after they handcuffed him?

Evidence Report
On March 1st 2011, the police let my dad and I go back to the house and they left the following as the Police Department Evidence Seizure List.

1. Shell Casing

2. Hammer

3. Shell Casing

4. WCSO Hat

5. Shell Casing

6. Live Round

7. Taser

8. Bullet Hole

9. Blood Spatter Swab

10. Blood Swab

11. Sunglasses

12. Taser AFIDS

13. Taser AFID by door

14. Blood Swab from bandages

15. Shell Casing

16. Taser Cartridge Door

17. Flashlight on table

18. WCSO deputy sleeve

19. Shell Casing

20. Shell Casing

21. Flashlight from Table

22. Pick Ax

23. Shell Casing

24. Shell Casing

25. Shell Casing

26. Shell Casing

27. Medications

28. Bullet

29. Shell Casing

30. Shell Casing

31. Shell Casing

32. Microwave

33. Flashlight

34. Hospital Documents

You will notice right away that on top of the seizure list was a Hammer. So basically when the detective came on scene, the officers' #1-4 must have told the detective where they "supposively" found a hammer. Of all the blood that was on the ground where my brother was dragged, of all the things that were laying in the garage, and all the bullets that were on the floor, they put "hammer" on the very top of the seizure list! Also they put stickers on the ground on where they found all the items, but they put the sticker of the "hammer" 13 feet away from my brother's body. My dad had three tool boxes in the garage and over $5000 dollars worth of tools. We had over four hammers in our tool boxes, but the police claim to only take one hammer that day. However, when we searched the entire garage, we couldn't find any of our hammers? We had to go to our neighbor's house to borrow a hammer so we could board up the house windows. Also there was a drawer and a lot of tool boxes in between my brother and where they supposively found a "hammer." If you counted the shell casings, there was 13 shots fired at my brother and there was ten bullets taken out of my brother's body.

The detective kept on calling my dad after my brother was murdered because he wanted to know what we saw. We kept on telling the detectives to come to the house so we could show them what happened, but one detective told us that he won't come to our house. So we told him, "If you don't come to our house then we won't talk to you until after the funeral." Then we had to wait until the autopsy was done on Alex and then wait until the doctor and the police to let Alex's body to us. Alex was murdered on a Monday and his body was released to us on a Friday so my sister paid the funeral company to transport his body from

Western Washington to Eastern Washington.

On Monday, March 7th 2011 was the day we could see Alex's body at the funeral. My uncle took me first to see my brother before everyone else, but when I walked inside the funeral building.... I saw Alex's body from a distance and then walked outside. I started to shake and I started to cry. Since my brother was murdered I haven't cried until that time. I was drinking through out the week and smoking all day long. I was so angry at the world and I wasn't crying during that time. However, when I saw Alex's body from a distance, I couldn't stop crying. My uncle tried to convince me to go inside the building to show my respect and to say good bye to my brother, but I couldn't do it. So my uncle decided to drive around and then we went to the store to buy a pack of cigarettes and two bottles of liquor. We started to drink and I still couldn't stop drinking. We went back to the funeral building an hour later.

A lot of people were inside the funeral building and outside the funeral building. That's when I saw my sister for the first time since Alex was murdered. We both hugged each other and we were crying for a long time. A lot of people were trying to get me inside the building to show my respect to Alex, but I couldn't go in there. I kept on telling everyone what I saw and every time I see my brother... All I see is him on the ground and the fucking cops shooting him! These fucking cops need to die and I want to fucking kill them! And I want them dead right fucking now!!! A lot of people couldn't feel my pain or feel my anger. They didn't see what I saw and didn't grow up with Alex. My dad started to cry too and he said, "I was there too and I know what you saw, but we have to be strong and say good bye to Alex." But I didn't want to say my good bye and I kept on telling people, "Tell Alex to come outside so we can go home, please tell Alex to walk outside so we can get out of here."

After a long time outside the funeral building, my family and friends finally convinced me to go inside to see Alex. When I finally started to walk towards Alex, I felt so dead inside. It felt like nothing was real and it seemed like nobody was feeling the pain that I was feeling. I was on my knees right next to Alex's body and face. I kept on talking to Alex... I kept on saying,

"Please Alex wake up, please Alex, you don't belong here!"

"I got the money so we could go to Mexico and never have to work again and we can leave this place right now and we don't ever have to talk to anyone else again!"

"So please Alex let's get out of here and never come back!"

"We can go to Mexico and go drink some Coronas at the beach and never have to do anything in life."

"I have the money so please wake up!"

"I am so sorry that the cops were shooting you when you were on the ground because I thought they were shooting bean bags or rubber bullets. If I knew they were real bullets, I would have killed all of them right there!" "I am so sorry because this is my fault and I should have driven you to the hospital!"

"I am so sorry that I failed you Alex and please tell me what I need to do so you can wake up?"

"I will do anything in life right now so you can walk out of this casket and we can go home!"

"Please Alex wake up, I told God that I am sacrificing my

soul so you can come back."

"I don't know what to do with my life and I need you to tell me what should I do?"

"I am going to kill these fucking cops and all the people who try to cover this up!"

"I swear to you and to God, if you don't wake up then I am going to kill a lot of these cops so please wake up."

"Please tell me what to do Alex, please tell me when or how do you want me to kill these cops?"

"Please Alex, get this pain out of me because it hurts too much, I am so sorry Alex, please forgive me."

"You don't belong here and I need you to wake up."

"Please Alex wake up, please Alex, you don't belong here!"

"I got the money so we could go to Mexico and never have to work again and we can leave this place right now and we don't ever have to talk to anyone else again!"

"So please Alex let's get out of here and never come back!"

"We can go to Mexico and go drink some Coronas at the beach and never have to do anything in life."

"I have the money so please wake up!"

"I am so sorry that the cops were shooting you when you were on the ground because I thought they were shooting bean bags or rubber bullets. If I knew they were real bullets, I would have killed all of them right there!" "I am so sorry because this is my fault and I should have driven you to the hospital!"

"I am so sorry that I failed you Alex and please tell me what I need to do so you can wake up?"

"I will do anything in life right now so you can walk out of this casket and we can go home!"

"Please Alex wake up, I told God that I am sacrificing my soul so you can come back"

"I don't know what to do with my life and I need you to tell me what should I do?"

"I am going to kill these fucking cops and all the people who try to cover this up!"

"I swear to you and to God, if you don't wake up then I am going to kill a lot of these cops so please wake up."

"Please tell me what to do Alex, please tell me when or how do you want me to kill these cops?"

"Please Alex, get this pain out of me because it hurts too much, I am so sorry Alex, please forgive me."

"You don't belong here and I need you to wake up."

"I am going to leave right now, but I will be back tomorrow."

"If you don't wake up, I am going to give up my soul so I know you are in Heaven with my mom, but I don't want you to go to Heaven, I want you to come back so we can kill these cops together and then we can go to Heaven together so please come back."

I was trying to wake my brother up for over an hour because I really thought he wasn't dead. Like I said before nothing made sense. When the cops shot Alex when he was on the ground because he had a flashlight and if they would have told the truth that they messed up because they thought he had a gun or a hammer then I would have accepted the fact that my brother was dead. However, since the cops were lying on what they did then I really thought my brother wasn't dead and that everything wasn't real. Because I saw it with my own two eyes on what happened and if it wasn't a horrible dream then it had to be something else? I really thought I was in HELL or some kind of cruel joke and I needed my brother to wake up.

After I finally left the funeral building that night, I just went back to my uncle's house to drink and pass out. The next day was when we had to bury my brother so I kept on hoping I would wake up out of my horrible nightmare. That night I was dreaming that Alex and I were in a car and Alex was driving the car down a hill going over 150 miles per hour. I was calm in the car because I was hanging out with my brother and he is the only person who I trust in this world. So after I woke up from my dream, I realized again that my brother was dead and that I had to bury his body.

We went back to the funeral building so people could talk about Alex and for one of our pastors to talk about Alex's life. There was a lot of family members and friends at Alex's funeral. I also made a speech about how much I cared about Alex and the things Alex did for me growing up. Then we had to take Alex to his burial site to bury him. We paid the funeral service to bury my brother right next to my mom's grave.

My dad, family members, and I had to carry my brother to his grave site. Do you know how it feels to carry your brother to his grave site after seeing him on the ground being shot non stop by the police? (This question is to the cops who murdered my brother and to the people who are trying to cover up his murder) "You have no clue who you killed and you have no clue what I can do! You have no clue on how much pain I am in and you have no clue on what I am going to do to you! Because I am going to make sure you feel my pain you piece of shit mother fuckers, you will feel my pain and you can't do anything to stop it!") Then everyone said their good-byes at the funeral, but I told my brother I wasn't saying good bye because I know I am going to see him again. I promised him I would see him again and that's when my brother's body was put into the ground.

After the funeral service, all my family members went to a local church to eat. I started to talk to my family members that I haven't seen for a long time. I told a lot of them that I was going to move back to Eastern Washington after I take care of some things back home. A lot of people were excited that I was going to live in Eastern Washington near my mom's side of the family. So after another day in Eastern Washington, I went back home so we could talk to the detective and so I could tell my job that I was going to quit.

I went back home on March 9th and we tried talking to the detective again. However, again he said that he won't come to our house because he said, "I don't need to come to your house and I won't come to your house!" So that is when we started to search for a lawyer so we could make this detective to do his job and to investigate my brother's murder. So after a week of looking for a lawyer, we finally found a good one. We talked to a lot of lawyers and a lot of the lawyers were talking about how much money they can get us or how cops can shoot a person 100 times if they feel threatened. My dad couldn't handle telling the story of what happened to his son because it's been too painful for him to say what happened. So when we found a good lawyer, he wasn't concerned about the money. He wanted the cops to eat their words and he wanted to make sure this doesn't happen again. That is the kind of lawyer I was looking for because I don't want a lawyer who only cares about the money, I want a lawyer that will make sure that the entire world knows the truth.

After we got our lawyer, we gave him the detective's phone number so he can make him come to the house. When our lawyer called me back, he told me that the detective said, "Well let me talk to a lawyer before I get back to you guys." So then I said, "Why the fuck does the detective need to talk to a lawyer? Isn't he a detective and isn't he suppose to do his job and not find a way to not come to our house?" Our lawyer was going to wait for his phone call and he would call me the next day. So the next day the detective called our lawyer and he said, "I am sorry, we got on the wrong foot here, but I am not coming to the house because I have pictures and videos of the house and I don't need to come to the house. It would be pointless for me to come to the house."

I was so pissed off after I heard that because I didn't understand why the detective didn't want to come to the house? I have pictures and videos of Mt. Everest, but if I don't go there then I won't know the difference. So we finally agreed to talk to the detective so he can finish his investigation, but only in our lawyer's office. We weren't going to see the detective until two weeks after my brother's funeral. During this time, my mind was getting a lot worst. When I was at work, I kept on thinking, "I need to kill these cops, I need to kill these cops now!" I even went to the hospital one day because I wanted to kill these cops, but at the same time I wanted to kill myself. So when it was the day to talk to the detective, I was really having a bad headache and smoking all morning.

When I sat down in the interview room, it was my lawyer and the detective with two other people. The detective wanted to shake my hand, but I didn't shake his hand because if I would have touched his hand, I probably would have started to punch him because he didn't want to come to my dad's house. So then I started to explain what happened that day as quickest as possible because I didn't want to be in that room. The detective gave me a white piece of paper like a school paper and he told me to show him how everything happened? How the hell was I going to show the detective how everything was placed in the garage, in that small piece of paper? So again I wanted to get out of that room because I knew if I stayed there too long, I would have tried to go after that detective. After the interview was over, I left and then my dad had to say what he saw. As soon as I left, I knew I didn't tell every single detail on what happened that day. So that is when I knew why the detective didn't want to come to the house.

The detective didn't want to come to our house for many reasons. However, the main reason why the detective didn't want to come to our house is because if he came to the house then we could show the detective inch by inch on where everything happened and where all items were in that garage. So the detective knew if he came to our house and we showed him the entire truth on what happened, he wouldn't be able to find a way to conclude on what we saw wasn't true. However, since he didn't come to our house and he made us try to explain what happened that day on a small piece of paper then he and the other officers have room to conclude that there were some similar things on what the police are saying what happened to our statements. In all serious, that interview was a complete waste of time.

The detective told us he wasn't on anybody's side, but after that day, I knew he was on the cop's side! (However, I will make sure that detective feels my pain, just wait mother fucker, you will get your turn!)

Dealing with the "Investigation"

We applied to get our funeral cost paid by the state even though we didn't need it, but it was a way to get the police report sooner than later. The detective kept on telling us that the investigation was still on going, but I knew that was bull shit because nobody was arrested and if nobody was arrested then I knew the police were calling us liars and that my brother's murder will not get any justice. So once I knew my brother wasn't going to get justice that's when I knew I had to do something about it. Remember.... They don't know who I am and they don't know what I am capable of doing so now I have no choice, but to reach out to some people who owe me some favors.

The first letter we got from the state:

March 17th, 2011

Dear Mr. Martinez:

Your application for benefits has been received. My staff and I are sorry to hear about your loss of your loved one. Please accept our sincere condolences.

You should hear from us in about 50 days regarding claim allowance. Enclosed is your brochure that tells you about the benefits our program can provide. To prevent undue hardship, the department may be to authorize burial expenses not to exceed the maximum allowable under law. In the event that any insurance, civil or court order recovery is made the department is required to seek reimbursement.

If you have any questions or concerns about your application, please call Customer Service Representative.

We waited to hear back from the state and it wasn't long until we heard from them because the detective kept on telling us that the investigation was still ongoing, but the state of Olympia sent us a new report.

May 6th, 2011

Mr. Martinez:

Please accept my condolences on the loss of your son.

I reviewed your application for crime victim's benefits. In order for a claim to be eligible for benefits, the victim cannot be engaged in an attempt to commit, or during the commission of, a felony.

When Mr. Perez-Martinez was shot, he was in the process of assaulting a law enforcement officer with a hammer.

I am sorry I was not able to make a different decision.

Sincerely,

Unit Supervisor

After I got this letter from the state, I called the Crime Victims Program and spoke to the Unit Supervisor. I asked her why the benefits were denied and she said it was because my brother was trying to assault an officer with a hammer? I told her that my dad and I were there and that didn't happen. So she advised me to write an appeal in order for them to change their decision. However, I asked her what evidence do you have or what kind of report do you have from the police so we can prove to you what happened. In order for us to prove to you what happened, we need to know what kind of lies the police are saying so we can show pictures, videos, and anything that is necessary so we can show our side of the story.

The Unit Supervisor said, "When I determine if a family is eligible for compensation, I get information from the police. In this case, I spoke to detective Blue and I asked him a list of questions. After the questions were answered from the detective, I have determined that the Crime Victim Program can not pay for any funeral expense." And I was shocked because I told her that my dad and I were there and saw what happened. So she kept repeating that I need to write an appeal, but like I said before I need their evidence so I can prove that their evidence is false and I can prove it wrong if they give me their report. She told me that she didn't have a report so that is when I get even more angrier because if she is only "Hearing" on the phone what the police are saying with no facts, with no evidence, and with no real investigation then she couldn't conclude that my family shouldn't be compensated for funeral expenses.

I don't even care about the funeral expense because everything has already been paid for the funeral, but I want that police report or any kind of cover up from the police so I can prove what they are doing is REALLY fucked up! However, again she advised us to write an appeal and again I said like before that I need actual evidence or a report. Also maybe she should actually do her job and investigate the case. But it seems like she doesn't do anything and she just sits on her chair at her job? If I had a state job and all I had to do was make some phone calls to gather evidence from a murder and not have one police report, not have pictures, not have video, and not do anything besides saying "Yes or No" then something is really wrong with this entire "Procedure." (And I am the one who will change this fucked up procedure!)

After we got the denial from the state, we contacted detective Mr. Blue again and he said, "The case is still under investigation and we have not concluded on what happened on February 28th 2011." Wait, wait one second here... If you haven't concluded on what happened on February 28th 2011 then why is the Unit Supervisor from Crime Victim's Program saying that the funeral expenses will not be paid? The Unit Supervisor told us that she got her information from (YOU, the detective who is investigating this case) so either she is lying or you, Detective Blue is lying. And to be 100% honest with you, I know Detective Blue is lying because his report was done and he kept on telling us that the investigation was still going so he could say, "We took our time doing this investigation and after X amount of months, we have concluded the following." However, I know the truth, his investigation was already over and he wants us to think he is still working on the case. He must not know that we spoke to the Unit Supervisor and know that he told her his conclusion.

Fuck this! Seriously fuck this Detective Mr. Blue. He thinks we are just some poor family that won't investigate and seek justice. He thinks I am a nobody and that I can't do anything about this. Well, Mr. Blue I am somebody that you are going to regret meeting and somebody you are going to regret lying to. You think you can play games with me and my family. You think I don't have the connections and know what to do so the truth will come out. Obviously you are wrong and you are going to lose something valuable. Just remember, I didn't choose your destiny, you chose to try to cover this up and not do your job and "Detect" this case.

During this time, I already quit my job and moved to Eastern Washington. I was living with my uncle during this time and then I found a job working at night as a cashier. However, I soon quit that job after two weeks because I kept on having issues. Every day while I was driving to work, I would cry, every day while I was at work, I would cry, and every day when I left work, I would cry and pound my hands on the steering wheel. I couldn't handle all my emotions so I had to quit working so I just stayed at my uncle's house to watch television. I would also go to church with my grandma and hang out with my uncle's family, but overall my mind was going crazy because I kept on reading the local news in Bellingham and I would never read, "The cops were arrested today for Alex's murder." I thought they would admit the truth or that the detective did his job and found the lies the cops did. However, every day that didn't happen, I just kept on getting worst and worst. So then our lawyer finally got the autopsy report and he let me have it in my request. He didn't want me to have, but I needed to read it. This is very specific and some readers will not stomach the conclusion so you can skip this section if you want.

Autopsy report

We got the autopsy report two months after my brother was murdered so this is when we found out how many times my brother was shot.

Name:	Martinez, Alex
Age:	30
Date of Death:	2/28/2011
Date of Autopsy:	3/01/2011
Investigating Agency:	Whatcom County
Sheriff Office	

Bellingham Police Department   Washington State Patrol

Autopsy Performed at: Whatcom County Morgue

Autopsy Ordered By: Whatcom County Medical Examiner

Autopsy Diagnosis

I.   Large Caliber (.40 ACP) gunshot wounds, right arm, chest, flank:

A. Perforations of right and left artria heart

B. Perforations of right lung

C. Right hemopneumothroax

D. Multiple right rib fractures, left intracostal hemorrhages

E. Maceration and disruption of right kidney

F. Perforations, maceration and disruption of right and left lobes of liver

G. Bullet inside spinal canal

H. Direction of fire (Right to left)

I. Range of fire: All indeterminate (no near contact or close range injuries)

J. 10 recovered bullets. 7 fired by WCSO, 3 by US Border Patrol

II.   History of remote cranial trauma

A. Multiple bone fasteners from remote craniotomy

B. Minimal architectural distortion of left cerebral cortex

C. Clinical history of mental health/behavioral abnormalities

III.   Remote scar, left lower lobe lung

IV.   Toxicology

A. Blood, urine and vitreous fluid alcohol: Negative

B. Blood drug screen: Not performed per WSTL protocol

C. Urine drug screen: Negative for drugs tested

D. Rapid Status DS urine drug screen: Negative for drugs tested

Cause of Death

Exsanguinations secondary to gunshot wounds to heart and right lung

Manner of Death:

Homicide

(This me writing again) You will notice from the diagnosis that the autopsy examiner couldn't determine "Range of fire?" I am really surprise because my dad and I were there and when the officers shot my brother, they were only three to five feet away from him so I don't understand why the autopsy examiner couldn't determine that? You will also notice that the autopsy examiner recovered 10 bullets from my brother's body. I believe the most important thing he put on the autopsy report so far is "Manner of Death" which was Homicide. However, some other people might think, the most important thing he put on the autopsy report so far is...... All drug and alcohol test came back were negative! Like I said before, my brother stopped doing drugs and alcohol a long time ago and he became a better person. He was a good person once again and these fucking cops are saying that he was and still is a criminal.

Clinical Summary:

The decedent is a 30 year old Hispanic Mexican male who

died after sustaining multiple, large caliber, handgun gunshot wounds in an altercation with law enforcement officers of the Whatcom County Sheriff's Office and Homeland Security (Border Patrol).

Preliminary information is that the decedent was acting in a violent and erratic manner, breaking windows of vehicles at his residence. Law enforcement responded after call from family members. The decedent was initially inside the residence and entered a carport area carrying a large hammer. He refused to release the weapon and when confronted by law enforcement, struck a WCSO deputy on the head causing significant and serious injuries. The decedent was tased once in the chest area with darts striking clothing. He failed to comply with law enforcement and subsequently was shot multiple times by an officer of the Border Patrol and a second WCSO deputy on scene. The injured deputy did not fire his weapon. The decedent was declared dead at the scene after being physically removed from the site of the shooting into an open area.

The altercation with law enforcement occurred in a small confined carport area restricted by vehicles and structure. Preliminary information suggests there were combined 13 fired shots. The Border Patrol Officer used an H&K .40 caliber ACP round and fired seven (7) times. Samples of the bullets were provided at my request and the rounds are distinguishable.

I (autopsy examiner) examined the decedent at the death scene and personally arranged for transportation to St. Joseph's Hospital for skeletal x-ray survey and localization of the projectiles. The body was then transported under MEO homicide protocol to the Whatcom county morgue and autopsy is performed on 3/01/2011 at 0800 hours with investigating officials WCSO Detective, BPD Detective, BPD CSI and Deputy Prosecutor in attendance. Under my direct supervision, the body was again transported the following day and re-x-rayed for location and subsequent removal of the fired bullets.

Identification:

No picture identification is found or with the body. Identification was established at the death scene and is not considered in question. Fingerprints are taken during the course of the autopsy.

(This is me George writing again) You will notice from the Clinical Summary report is full of lies! First of all, I don't understand why the autopsy examiner is putting what the police are saying what happened at my dad's house in the autopsy report? Why does the autopsy examiner need to put what the police are saying? What else are the police telling the autopsy examiner to put in his report? The other thing I don't understand is, the autopsy examiner says my brother was tased in the chest area once, but my dad and I were in the garage or (carport) and saw the police didn't tase my brother. Also when I was giving my brother CPR, Alex didn't have any tasers on his clothing or his chest so this really pisses me off! Either the police told the autopsy examiner to put my brother was tased or, officer #1, officer #2, or officer #3 tased my brother after they threw my dad and I out of the garage! Wow, I was so pissed off when I found out that they are saying my brother was tased in the autopsy report because they have no clue that there lies will come back to them and they don't know who they are dealing with.

The other thing that pisses me off is because now they

are saying my brother came out walking and they instructed my brother to release the hammer in his hand? Well, first of all he didn't have a hammer and second, the only thing the cops said that day was, "Alex come out of the house." So if the cops are saying Alex had a hammer in his hand and they instructed him to release the weapon, how did my brother hit the officer in the head with the hammer? If I saw someone with a hammer and I told that person to release the weapon, I wouldn't just stand there and let the person hit me in the head with a hammer... So again, "How did my brother have a hammer and how did he go towards a cop with three other police officers behind him to get hit with a hammer on the head?" I don't know about you, but I think that entire story was bullshit! If you read the report the previous day, the police said, "Alex ran out of the house swinging a hammer and that he hit an officer in the head with a hammer, but now they changed their story." I was so shocked that they changed their story because I thought their story would be somewhat similar to their story the previous day and now they changed their entire story.

The other thing I don't understand is the autopsy examiner said, "Alex struck a WCSO deputy on the head causing significant and serious injuries?" That does not make sense because I saw that officer on the ground and he kept on telling everyone, "I am ok, I am ok." And in the news report and in the press conference they said the struck officer was conscious and ok. They even said he would be released from the hospital that same day, but they wanted to keep him over night for examination, but overall he was doing ok and nothing major was wrong with him. So I am assuming after the cops realized how bad they fucked up and how many times they shot my brother on the ground, they want to make it seem like the injured deputy was seriously injured so they can say, "We had no choice, but to shoot Alex 13 times!" Do you guys (the reader) understand why the cops are changing their story yet? Do you really think they want to admit they fucked up and told everyone on T.V. that they lied and that they really fucked up?

The last thing I don't understand on the Clinical Summary is.... the autopsy examiner reported, "The alteration with law enforcement occurred in a small confined carport area restricted by vehicles and structure." So if the alteration occurred in a small confined area in the carport/garage, why did the autopsy examiner put in the beginning of his autopsy report "Range of fire: All indeterminate (no near contact or close range injuries)? How can the autopsy examiner say the carport/garage is a small confined area, but he can't determine how close the shootings were? Is it because the police don't want him to show how close the shots were because then people will understand the truth.... The truth is my brother was shot at 13 times when the police were only three to five feet away from him! We should have gotten a private autopsy report, but we were too devastated on what happened so we just wanted to get the funeral done as soon as possible.

So now I am going to put the rest of the autopsy report and I will not say anything until the end of the report.

External Identifying Marks:

1. Professionally made tattoo in uniform dark colored ink in cursive writing "Jazmin", with a heart above the letter "i", located superior and medical to the left nipple on the left upper chest.

2. Homemade style dot tattoo on the lateral left wrist.

3. Homemade style tattoo of perhaps a cat face on the distal right anterior thigh in uniform dark colored ink.

4. Hypopigmented ancient scars overly the distal and posterior-lateral aspects of the right patella, 2.6 x 2.4 and 2.7 x 1.8 cm.

5. Faint, vertically oriented linear incision scar on the distal anterior-lateral left upper arm, 2.3 x 0.1 cm.

Note: Most major, but possibly not all tattoos and scars are documented.

Personal Effects:

No personal effects of value are found on or with the decedent.

Clothing:

1. In place on the lower body are moderately worn green denim jeans, brand Dickies, size 36 x 30. Pockets are empty. Closing the waistline is well worn brown leather belt with silver colored rectangular belt buckle, brand Fossil "Fuel".

2. On the torso is a medium weight black jacket, brand Weatherproof size indeterminate. Pockets are empty.

3. On the torso is an orange cotton T shirt, well worn, brand South Pole, size XL, with worn decal on the anterior fabric, "South Pole".

4. On the decedent's feet are heavily soiled, well worn, upper calf height, white cotton socks, one brand Hanes and the other champion.

5. On the decedent's feet are gray, moderately worn, ankle height athletic style shoes, brand Nike, size US 10.5. Both shoes are untied but with closed Velcro straps. The soles contain copious brown muddy fluid and occasional

embedded shards of glass (decedent walked in broken auto glass).

Perforations of Clothing:

Note: The numbering of the perforations is associated only with each individual garment and not intended to reflect numbered perforations on skin of the body.

Pants: (Range of fire of perforations is considered "indeterminate" based on lack of powder, soot, gunshot residue).

1. Fabric perforation with frayed edges 2.0 cm distal to the 2nd belt loop on right side, 5.0 cm from top of pants, immediately adjacent to the lateral inseam.

2, 3. Perforations of the right anterior pocket, located immediately distal to the pocket seam in the mid portion of the pocket, 10.0 cm from the top of the pants. These two perforations appear associated with the same projectile.

T-Shirt: (Range of fire of perforations is considered "indeterminate" based on lack of powder, soot, gunshot residue.)

1,2. At the periphery of the sleeve and 4.0 cm from the sleeve margin, are two perforations with ragged margins, both 1.4 x 1.2 cm, located 7.0 cm from the axillary seam.

3. 7.0 cm distal to the axilla is a perforation with ragged margins.

4. Located immediately above the letter "O" of the anterior chest decal on the right lower chest region, located 13.5 cm from the lateral margin, 36.0 cm from the waist margin, 0.8 x 0.6 cm, is a ragged perforation.

5. Located 5.5 cm from the right lateral margin is an oval

perforation, 23.0 cm above the distal edge of the fabric, without jagged tearing of the margin, 2.1 x 2.0 cm.

6. Located 2.5 cm transversely from #5, is a round perforation, 2.0 x 2.2 cm, without jagged peripheral margin, located 3.4 cm from the lateral fabric margin and 20.5 cm from the distal seam.

7. On the lower back at the seam is a round perforation, 0.6 x 0.5 cm, located 21.3 cm from the right lateral margin.

8. Oval perforation without tearing at the periphery on the right lower back, 1.5 x 0.9 cm, located 8.5 cm from the distal seam and 14.5 cm from the lateral edge of the fabric.

9. Associated with #6 above is a transversely oriented perforation without fraying of the peripheral margin, located 18.8 cm above the distal seam and 3.0 cm from the lateral margin.

10. Located 16.5 cm from the distal seam, 4.5 cm from the lateral margin, is a round perforation, 0.8 x 0.6 cm.

11. On the mid right back is a horizontally oriented fabric defect, clean at the margins, 2.0 x 1.2 cm, located 10.5 cm from the lateral margin, 39 cm from the shoulder.

12. Round perforation with fraying at the margins, 0.8 x 0.7 cm, located 13.0 from there lateral seam and 38 cm from the shoulder.

13. Oval horizontal defect in the fabric of the midline back, 3.7 x 1.5 cm, located 23.5 cm from the lateral margin and 38 cm from the shoulder.

Taser Darts: (Stuck in Jacket fabric)

1. One taser dart is located in the fabric on the left side of the jacket zipper, located 26.5 cm above the jacket and 2.5

cm left of the zipper.

2. The second taser dart is located 41.0 cm above the bottom of the jacket and 2.5 cm left of the midline

3. Neither taser is attached to its guide wire. Both are removed from the jacket and preserved.

Jacket: (Range of fire of perforations is considered "indeterminate" based on lack of powder, soot, gunshot residue).

1. 17.5 cm lateral to the anterior zipper, 27.5 cm above the bottom seam of the fabric, is a perforation with jagged margin through the right anterior pocket, 1.2 x 0.8 cm.

2. Posterior to the pocket, 4.0 cm anterior to the lateral inseam, 14.5 cm from the bottom of the jacket is a round perforation 0.8 x 0.8 cm.

3. Through the axilla is a jagged perforation, 3.5 cm anterior to the medial seam, 39.5 cm from the bottom of the jacket, 2.8 x 1.7 cm.

4. 13.7 cm proximal to the cuff on the right sleeve, 4.0 cm posterior to the midline hem, is a perforation 1.8 x 1.4 cm.

5. 4.2 cm anterior to the seam, 26.0 cm from the cuff, is a perforation 1.2 x 1.0 cm.

6. 16.0 cm anterior to the midline cuff, 32.0 cm from the sleeve is a perforation 1.2 x 1.0 cm.

7. 1.5 cm from the sleeve seam to the body, 4.0 cm anterior to the axillary hem, is a perforation 1.5 x 1.0 cm. Note: Likely associated with #5 above.

8. 22.0 cm anterior to the axillary seam, 30.0 cm from the cuff, is a perforation 1.2 x 1.0 cm.

9-17. On the posterior lateral panel of the jacket are

individual perforations between 3.0 and 1.2 cm in greatest dimension.

18-22. All perforations through the back of the jacket and individually measuring between 4.0 and 1.5 cm.

Note: Documentation of clothing perforations is best visualized by review of photos taken by BPD after drying of the articles. These photos are appended to the autopsy record and were taken at my request.

External Evidence of Law Enforcement Activity:

1. Bullet wounds are separately described.

2. The decedent is hand cuffed with wrists behind his back. There are impressions on both wrists from the cuffs without epidermal abrasion, fractures or other significant injuries.

3. Expended Taser darts (2) are stuck to the outer coat garment near the midline anterior left vertical zipper hem.

External Evidence of Medical Therapy:

A bandage was placed over some of the chest bullet perforations at the death scene. There are no other external artifacts of attempted resuscitation. The body was previously placed on a body board and moved approximately 40 feet from the reported site of the shooting to an open location for medical assessment. The body was not further manipulated prior to my on site examination.

External Evidence of Injury:

1. Very superficial epidermal abrasion superior and lateral to the right eyebrow on the right temporal forehead, 0.8 x 0.6 cm, pink in color (likely an antemortem injury)

2. There is a superficial oval scrape abrasion with dry

orange-tan epidermis, lateral to the right patella, 1.8 x 1.4 cm (likely a postmortem injury).

Gunshot perforations:

The decedent has numerous gunshot perforations, all consistent with large caliber handgun injuries, involving the right axilla, right torso, right flank, right arm and right back. There are no injuries to the cranium and there are no injuries below mid thighs. The injuries are sequentially numbered without initial regard for entrance/exit. The numbers below correspond to the number of the wound written on the body.

Note: The nipples lay 138.3 cm above the right heel and 12.6 cm lateral to the midline of the chest. All measurements are taken from the approximate center of the skin perforations.

#1. Right axilla, 144.6 cm above the right heel, 10.7 cm lateral and 4.8 cm superior to the right nipple, with protrusion of a fragment of bullet in the opening. There is a faint abrasion collar on the inferior margin. The perforation diameter is 1.7 x 1.2 cm.

#2. Gunshot wound entrance with a peripheral rim of burning, oval skin perforation, located 135.3 cm superior to the right heel, 13.1 cm lateral and 4.2 cm inferior to the right nipple. The skin injury measures 2.6 x 1.8 cm with peripheral burning on the external surface up to 0.4 cm. The projectile perforation diameter is 0.8 x 0.4 cm.

#3. Gunshot wound entrance on the lower right chest, oval, abrasion collar at the periphery, burning at the periphery, located 124.8 cm above the right heel, 13.1 cm inferior and 1.4 cm lateral to the right nipple. The perforation diameter is 2.1 x 1.6 cm.

#4. Vertically oriented, probable gunshot wound of entrance, on the lateral inferior right chest, located 121.6 cm above the right heel, 4.6 cm lateral and 16.3 cm distal to the right nipple. There is a faint abrasion collar on the superior and anterior margins and grazing abrasion on the inferior margin of the injury. The perforation diameter is 2.3 x 1.7 cm.

#5. Located in the right axillary line of the lower right chest is a vertically oriented gunshot wound of entrance, located 118.9 cm above the right heel, 11.6 cm lateral and 18.0 cm distal to the right nipple. There is burning present circumferentially about the skin perforation with maximum 0.8 cm width. The perforation diameter is 1.6 x 1.2 cm.

#6. Overlying the right hip is an oval to stellate gunshot wound of entrance, located 103.8 cm above the right heel, 14.8 cm lateral and 24.0 distal to the right nipple. The skin perforation measures 2.3 x 2.0 cm and has burning at the superior and anterior margins. No obvious abrasion collar. The perforation diameter is 2.0 x 1.9 cm.

#7. Oval skin defect is located 106.0 cm above the right heel on the lateral right buttocks, 21.5 cm lateral and 30.0 cm distal to the right nipple. The perforation diameter is 1.2 x 0.8 cm and there is no obvious abrasion collar or burning at the peripheral margin.

#8. Transversely oriented perforation of the lateral right hip, located 99.7 cm above the right heel, 18.3 cm lateral and 28.0 cm distal to the right nipple. The wound is probably an entrance with a small area of burning at the superior margin and perhaps a slight abrasion collar at the superior margin. The perforation measures 1.5 x 1.2 cm.

#9. Located 90.3 cm above the right heel, 13.0 cm lateral

and 48.0 cm distal to the right nipple, is a vertically oriented gunshot wound entrance with distinct burning at the distal and lateral margins and a clear abrasion collar at the periphery. The perforation measures 1.2 x 1.1 cm.

#10. On the posterior lateral right buttocks is a transversely oriented gunshot wound of entrance, 95.6 cm above the right heel, 22.0 cm lateral and 43.0 cm distal to the right nipple. There is a faint abrasion collar on the superior and anterior margins of the perforation which measure 2.0 x 1.8 cm.

#11. On the posterior lateral right chest is a gunshot wound of entrance, located 130.6 cm above the right heel, 19.5 cm lateral and 7.5 cm distal to the right nipple. The perforation is horizontally oriented with burning and an abrasion collar on the anterior margin. The perforation measures 2.8 x 1.7 cm.

#12. On the lateral right arm proximal to the elbow, located 133.0 cm above the right heel, 8.0 cm anterior and 3.5 cm proximal to the point of the elbow, is a vertically oriented slit-like perforation, probably a wound of exit, measuring 2.2 x 1.3 cm. There are radial tears at the periphery of the perforation. There is no burning, soot, abrasion collar or other transferred material.

#13. Located 134.5 cm above the right heel on the anterior distal right upper arm is a transversely oriented perforation, likely an exit, measuring 2.2 x 1.3 cm. Fat extrudes from the injury. The skin periphery is rough with small radial tears, no soot or smoke, no abrasion collar and no burning.

#14. On the medial right upper arm distal to the axilla, located 138.0 cm above the right heel, is a horizontally oriented skin perforation, probably an exit, without soot, smoke, abrasion collar or burning of the periphery. The perforation measures 2.2 x 0.9 cm.

#15. Located 126.3 cm above the right heel is a round perforation of the right mid back, 12.5 cm lateral to the midline of the back, 2.4 x 2.0 cm. There are small radial tears at the periphery. There is no abrasion collar, soot, smoke or burning at the periphery.

#16. Located 124.3 cm above the right heel, 13.5 cm right of the midline of the back, is a round skin perforation, 1.0 x 0.9 cm, with an epidermal abrasion at the periphery extending 1.9 x 1.7 cm. This is not an abrasion collar but rather denuded epidermis. There is no burning, soot, smoke or internal abrasion of the periphery margin.

#17. Located 93.5 cm above the right heel is a punched out appearing oval skin defect, 1.2 x 0.9 cm, without obvious abrasion collar. There is no soot, burning or other transferred material at the margin.

#18. Without skin perforation, located 88.0 cm above the right heel, is a small dimple with faint pink coloration. There is a firm structure below the skin which represents a retained bullet in the buttock.

General External Examination:

The decedent is a muscular, well developed and well nourished adult Hispanic male appearing younger than reported age. The body measures 70 inches in length and weighs an estimated 185 pounds. The body is cool following overnight refrigeration. Rigor is 3-4+ in the extremities and lower jaw. Lividity is dorsal and nearly fixed. The body does not smell of ethanol coginers or other foreign substances. Skin hygiene is considered average. There is copious vomit and blood exiting the nares and mouth staining the face, cheeks and ears. No blood is present in the internal ear canals. Head hair is black, straight and of average 5-7 cm length. There is no male pattern hair loss and there are no gray hairs. Eyebrows are uniform black in color and of moderate thickness. Ears are normal placed with symmetrical lividity, blood staining both moderate thickness. Ears are normally placed with symmetrical lividity, blood staining both pinnae but absence of blood in the ear canals. Earlobes are not pierced. Retroauricular areas are unremarkable. Sclerae are white. Iris color is brown. Pupils are round and symmetrical with conjugate gaze. There are no conjuctival petechial hemorrhages. The decedent has tache noire. Palpation of the nose and anterior facial sinuses reveals no cartilaginous or bony traumatic injuries. The nares and mouth weep vomit and blood. The decedent has natural teeth in the upper and lower jaws. Teeth are intact. The decedent does not appear to have had prior orthodonture. There are superficial epidermal abrasions from bite injuries to the upper and lower lips. He has male pattern facial hair in usual distribution of 3-7 mm length. The neck is supple without external injury. The chest is symmetrical. The right arm is fractured secondary to gunshot wounds in the mid and distal humerus above the elbow. Hands are dirty but soft. No combative or defensive wounds to the hands are evident. Fingernails and toe nails are of average length. No needle tracks are apparent. The abdomen is soft and doughy. The genitalia are those of a non-circumcised adult male with usual secondary sexual development. Both testicles lie within the scrotum and there are no palpable masses or cysts. Examination of the back is remarkable for the bullet perforations. There are no additional traumatic injuries. The decedent has no obvious combative or defensive injuries.

Internal Evidence of Injury:

1. Right 5th rib fractures at costochondral junction.

2. right 10th - 12th rib fractures lateral to costochondral junction.

3. Left 3rd - 4th rib fractures with perforation between intercostal muscles.

4. Two perforations of heart: Right and left atria.

5. Right hemopneumothroax.

6. Three perforation of right lung.

7. Perforation and maceration of right and left lobes of liver.

8. Maceration of hilar and posterior right kidney.

9. Fractures of mid and distal right humerus (compound, complex).

10. Ten bullets are recovered:

      A. Right buttock associated with skin perforation #18

      B. Subcutaneous tissue of axilla associated with perforation #1

      C. Right anterior chest

      D. Right back in proximal psoas muscle

      E. Left chest

      F. Right hilum of lung

      G. Associated with right kidney

      H. Right upper neck

      I. Lumbar vertebral body, deeply embedded

      J. In the spinal canal of the thoracic vertebral

column, mobile

11. Based on the characteristics of the bullets listed in #10 above: A. B, D, E, H, I and J are rounds from the sheriff's office while C, F and G are rounds from the Border Patrol.

General Internal Examination:

The skin of the chest and abdomen is reflected with a Y incision in the usual manner and the rib plate is removed revealing a collapsed right lung and right hemopneumothorax. Due to the multiple bullets, following individual tracks is difficult. There is estimated 450 cc of blood in the right chest. Internal organs are pale and bloodless. The heart, right lung, right kidney and liver are heavily damaged.

Clear yellow urine is collected from the urinary bladder, blood from the right chest (little blood remains in vascular compartment) and vitreous fluid from the eyes. There is no gastrointestinal contamination of blood. Gastric contents are also saved.

Heart: The heart weighs 345 gm and has large perforations through the right and left atria. There are associated pericardial perforations. The heart is of normal size and anatomy. Left and right ventricular wall thickness considered normal and there are no myocardial scars. Cardiac valves show normal morphology and are free of vegations. Coronary arteries arise in the usual manner and contain fatty streaks but no significant luminal occlusions. The aorta arises in the usual manner and is intact. Blood in the vascular compartment is minimal.

Respiratory system: The right lung weighs 355gm and left lung 350 gm. There is an old scar in the left lower lobe of lung. There are multiple bullet perforations, at least three, of the right upper and middle lobes of lung. The decedent has aspirated blood into both lungs. The right lung is collapsed. A bullet is recovered at the right hilum. There is increased carbon in pleural lymphatics and hilar lymph nodes consistent with tobacco usage.

Gastrointestinal tract: The esophageal mucosa is intact and remarkable. The stomach contains yellow mushy gastric contents without recognizable food particles or pill fragments. A sample of gastric contents is retained. Stool is soft. There is no blood in the stomach or intestines. There are no GI perforations or traumatic injuries. The appendix is present.

Liver: The liver weighs 1,400 gm and appears pale and bloodless. There are large zones of tissue disruption associated with bullet damage at both the right and left lobes of liver. Hepatocytes and bile ducts are otherwise unremarkable. There is no suspected increase in fibrous connective tissue. The gallbladder is either absent or was disrupted by the projectiles. There is no free bile in the abdominal cavity.

Spleen: The spleen weighs 185 gm and shows no traumatic injury. The organ appears pale and bloodless. There are no tumors.

Urinary tract: The right and left kidneys each weigh 165 gm. The posterior and hilar surfaces of the right kidney are disrupted with tissue maceration. A bullet is found in association with this injury. There is minimal blood in the right retroperitoneum despite extensive damage to the kidney.

Endocrine organs: The adrenals, pancreas and thyroid are unremarkable.

Reticuloendothelial system: No enlarged or suspicious lymph nodes are evident.

Neck: There are no traumatic injuries to cartilaginous or bony structures of the neck. A bullet is found in the upper neck adjacent to the undamaged right carotid artery. There are no hemorrhages in soft tissue of the neck.

Head: The scalp is reflected in the usual manner and there are no subcalpular hemorrhages. The convexity of the skull is removed in the usual manner avoiding the multiple bone fasteners from remote craniotomy. There are mild anatomical abnormalities of the convexity of the brain without formation of a finite cystic cavity. Gross examination of the brain is nearly normal and unremarkable. Ventricles are symmetrical in size. There is no midline shift. There is no obvious gross brain deformity.

Microscopic:

Heart: Perforations of the right and left ventricle are associated with hemorrhage. The myocardium has normal underlying histology without pathological alteration.

Lungs: Architectural collapse associated with parenchymal hemorrhages.

Liver: Mild steatosis, estimated at <10% of hepatocytes. Mild chronic inflammation, non-specific pattern.

Spleen: Paucity of blood in red pulp as evidence of agonal exsanguinations.

Kidney: The non-traumatized kidney shows no pathological abnormalities.

Brain: Section of hippocampus with no pathological abnormalities.

Toxicology:

Blood, urine and vitreous alcohol determination yield negative results.

Blood drug screen by the Washington State Toxicology Laboratory is not performed per their protocol.

Urine drug screen by the Washington State Toxicology Laboratory is negative for amphetamines, barbiturates, benzodiazepines, cannabinoids, cocaine, opiates, phencyclidine, methadone, propoxphene and tricyclic antidepressants.

Urine drug screen by Lab Corp using immunoassay methodology is negative for metabolites of amphetamines, barbiturates, benzodiazepines, cannabinoids, cocaine, opiates, phencyclidine, methadone and propoxphene.

Rapid Status DS drug screen yields no drugs detected.

After reading the rest of the autopsy report you will notice a lot of horrible things on what happened to my brother. One of the most important things you will notice that the autopsy said, "The decedent has no obvious combative or defensive injuries." Which is actually make sense because like I said from the beginning after the first shot, my brother fell onto the ground and the police officers kept on shooting him. So if my brother was attacking an officer with a hammer and then he got shot, he would have combative or defensive injuries to protect himself. But since he fell right after the first shot, he couldn't defend himself because he was on the ground when the police kept on shooting him.

The other thing that is important is when the autopsy examiner said, "A bandage was placed over some of the chest bullet perforations at the death scene and there are no other external artifacts of attempted resuscitation." The day of the incident, the police said that they tried to give my brother CPR, but I was there and that was bullshit. The only person who tried to give Alex CPR was me and the only thing they did for him was put a thing on his mouth for a couple of seconds and then checked his eyes. After that, they determined he was dead. So if the police are saying they gave my brother CPR then why is the autopsy examiner saying that there are no other external artifacts of attempted resuscitation? It's because they are trying to say that they followed "Police procedure" but everything they did that day was a complete "Fuck Up" and it seemed like all the police who were on that scene didn't have any police training. If they are saying they followed police procedure then they need to have a new police procedure!

The autopsy examiner put in great detail on where all 10 bullets were recovered from my brother. It really sucks that my brother was shot so many times, but at the same time these police are not trained properly and a lot of the people need to realize the truth! So at the end of the book you will understand why I wrote this book.

The autopsy examiner even sent out my brother's urine to other associates and they all concluded my brother wasn't doing any type of drugs. My brother didn't even have any alcohol in his system either because like I said before, my brother changed and he was a good person again. However, these piece of shit cops, didn't know what they were doing and they have no clue on what I am going to do to them!

And now it's the waiting game...... Because since February 28th 2011, we have been waiting day by day, hour by hour, minute by minute, second by second on what the police are finally going to say? We want to see and hear on what their final police report is going to say, but I know they won't tell the truth and do the right thing. They will still try to explain to the world that my brother had a hammer and to make it even worse, they are calling my dad and I, "Liars."

So again Thank you again (Police) for calling my dad and I liars and basically calling us criminals!

Why did you murdered my brother!

The real question should be.... Why did you shoot my brother? The pain doesn't want to leave my mind, my body, and my soul because it just stays there thinking of the same thing over and over again. The question that has changed my life for eternity, the question that has made me change to become the person of today. The question that thrives me to do things in life the way I have never thought of before, the question that I won't ever forget! "Why did you murder my brother?" Quit fucking lying and tell me the truth! What did my brother do to deserve this? Why did you keep shooting my brother when he was on the ground? He didn't have a hammer! Alex never ran out of the house swinging a hammer in order for you to start shooting him! I always tried to do the right thing in life and I have no clue why you shot my brother and the only response you told me in that garage was (Police officer #2) said, "I thought he had a hammer." You just stood there with your eyes wide open and your gun still pointing at my brother thinking, "Holy shit, what did we do?" I don't want any fucking money, I want my brother to be by my side right now! So why don't you tell me the truth and tell me why you shot my brother? FUCK, WHY DID THIS HAPPEN TO MY BROTHER?

I know now that this pain won't ever go away no matter what I do in life, it's going to be with me for the rest of eternity. You are going to read on what I had and what I have now and you will see that it won't ever get better again. No matter what I do from now on, no matter how much money I have or don't have, I will never feel anything that will make my life any better. However, the only thing that I will feel is like dying every second of my life and I can't do anything to stop it.

Every where I am at, either it's with my friends, family or being alone, jogging, working out, I keep on thinking "WHY" and how did this happen to my brother! I never hit an officer in my life, but right now I know my future.... That future is going to make these officer's feel my pain!

I always tried to be there for my brother so he could try to live a normal life so why did this happen to my brother? If anything, he deserves anything but this! He made me a great person and I did everything right in life except for a few mistakes that made me become a better person in life. And I am a very unique person, I do so much in my life to help others and I am always looking for the right thing to do. So how could something so terrible in my life happen to my brother and I?

I had so many other bad experiences that some people might think is worst than the situation that I am going through every second of my life for example Alex was hit with a baseball bat over ten years ago. Also his ex-girlfriend took away his only child because he wasn't mentally fit to have custody of his child and he used drugs a long time ago, but he quit doing drugs and alcohol! And I did anything that was possible for my brother so he could live with me and have anything that he wanted in life. I will admit my brother had some drug and temper problems in the past, but he volunteered himself in a rehab center to make his life better and to get his child back so the child can have a better life with him too. However, the courts don't look at what he has accomplished, they just look at his past and how much he spent on his lawyer.

I have so many other bad experiences in my life that no

ordinary person could handle, like my brothers, friends and I were shot by a Nazi with a machine gun while I was only eight years old and then we had to deal with all the racist people around us while we were growing up as a kid. There were so many racist people in the city where I grew up as a kid that it made it really hard for myself, my friends, and my family members to get a job. That is why my dad moved us away from all that to a better city, but now that my brother was murdered in that city by these fucking coward and corrupted cops... Well now my dad will understand it was a mistake to live in that city! We couldn't do anything without a person who didn't know us of accusing us of a crime even with no evidence linking us to the crime. We had to hear a racist remark at least three times a week, but it didn't bother my brother and I. My brother Alex taught me that there is only one race in this world and that is the human race. However, I do know it bothered some of my family members and friends so I tried to help them understand that no matter how much anger they have, they needed to let it go because the people who call us names are not educated enough and are just threatened that we will be better than them.

The other bad experience was my mom died when I was a just a baby. I was two years old when my mom died so I never got to know her. I always tried to do good things in my life so I get to see her in Heaven. I don't go to church every week and I don't pray every day, but I do believe if I do good things than I should go to Heaven. Also my mom's side of the family blame my dad for my mom's death because he moved us to another city so they haven't spoken to him after she died. (Well now since my brother was murdered, they finally saw him at the funeral.)

I tried my best to do everything right in life and I never physically hurt anyone unless they tried to hurt me growing up. There is no reason in this world on why my brother deserves this pain and there is no reason why I deserve this pain! I always helped people around me even if they didn't want my help. I was doing so great in life by helping my brother live his life before everything fell apart. I became a role model for a lot of the kids who I hanged out with. However, mostly everyone didn't know who I really was because I had a different life than they really knew. Everyone knew me because of my superior athletic skills. My entire childhood should have been great for my brother and I, but everything we did together was taken away from us when he was hit with a baseball bat and then eventually murdered.

Our entire life growing up, we had everything kids would want, but now I keep on asking myself..... "Why did you murder my brother?" I was the fastest kid, a smart kid, a popular kid, I had it all because my brother Alex helped me out so much growing up. However, now I am not even sort of satisfied with my life because everything that I do have or don't have is taken away from me and these corrupted cops are lying about everything. So now I am wondering what the fuck am I going to do now? I keep on asking myself that question because everything that I had and everything that I did with my brother is taken away from me! And now every second of my life I see my brother on the ground getting shot by these stupid mother fucking cops 13 times!!!! The autopsy doctor took out 10 fucking bullets out of him!!! Everyone tells me that I am living in Hell on earth, but if this is really earth and if this is really happening than why are these cops still lying and telling everyone that my brother had a hammer? So I promised my brother and myself that I will wait to see if these cops go to jail because if they don't than I have to do something about it!

Come on God, bring my brother back so I can be happy again because if he is really dead and if these cops really slaughtered my brother for no reason than you know what I am going to do and I will have no problem doing what I need to do!

One night after the funeral when I was praying to God to help me find something to make me live in peace, I said, "God if you can put your hands on these cops to tell the truth, I will do anything that you want me to do to so I can live my life in peace. I know if these cops tell the truth, it will make me understand that I am not in HELL and that I am on Earth and that these cops over reacted and murdered my brother by accident. Just like they almost murdered me when I grabbed my cell phone to call 911 again, but they kept on yelling at me to throw my gun on the ground? What fucking gun? I had my cell phone and they kept on yelling at me to throw down my gun? If I didn't jump on the ground and hide underneath my dad's truck, they would have killed me and they probably would have placed a gun on the scene too! However, if they keep on telling lies than I will know I am in HELL and you know what I am capable of doing and I will have no choice, but to show these cops my pain so they can FEEL my pain. "I will sacrifice everything and anything so these cops can tell the truth that my brother didn't have a hammer and that he had a flashlight." "I will be a good person for my eternal life so I can prove to you that I do have a good soul for eternity." "Please God convince these cops to tell the truth, Amen."

My dad use to take our family to church every Sunday,

but I was never really religious growing up. However, I do try to do the right things in life and I do believe if I do the right things that I would see my mom in Heaven one day and now my brother Alex too. My dad is very religious, he always has a bible in his vehicle, he prays every day, he goes to church every week, but at the same time he has made a lot of mistakes in his past too. However, if you met him and you see what he does every day than you will have no doubt that he is telling the truth on what happened to my brother.

You don't know how much pain I have been suffering since that moment I saw my brother lying on the ground while the cops kept on shooting him! I will never be the same person that I once was before. I want to punch walls, hit people, and yell as hard as I can to let this pain go away! Because that is what we do, right? To let the pain go away after we get stung by a bee, hit by a ball, or get your heart broken. We have to let our emotions out, right? But after we get it out.... Doesn't it have to leave and not hurt anymore? Then why is it still hurting me and sometimes it hurts so much that I can't think of anything else, except for the pain that I am going through. My heart beats faster, my head gets bad migraines, and my body tends to have this little twitch once in a while.

I have been to the hospital a few times because I thought I was having a heart attack, but it was just panic attacks. I am trying so-so hard to stop this pain, but I can't find anything to make myself stop thinking "Why did you murder my brother so brutally?" I can't stop thinking about all the good times we had together and all the times I felt so happy hanging out with my brother. I felt so "happy hanging out with my brother," it was so great I can't even explain that feeling. All I had growing up was my brother

Alex because my oldest sister lived with my aunt and uncles in Eastern Washington. Also my oldest brother moved to Eastern Washington when he was a kid, while my dad worked all the time until he remarried and started his new family. Alex and I would always hang out together because that is all we had. We just had each other and he taught me everything in life. I wish I could show the world on everything Alex did for me, but I can't show you every second. I wish I could have my brother for another second and not having the last seconds of his life...... of him lying on the ground with all those bullets in him and while I was giving him CPR and then getting tackled off him! What kind of Police Officer tackles a person giving another person CPR?

Just imagine the happiest day of your life, well I felt that way all the time with my brother because nothing in the world could make me unhappy when I was hanging out with my brother. I am not making up my feelings because when I was with Alex, I didn't care if we had no money or had millions of dollars! We knew that all we had was each other and we would always hang out with each other because we relied on each other to get through life.

I have tried to go out every day to make myself function in life, but nothing is working! I quit my job because my mind kept on thinking of what I was going through and I kept on hearing, "You gotta kill these piece of shit cops, You gotta kill these cops, come on man kill these fucking cops!" So then I would tell myself, "Yes, I will kill these cops and all the people who are trying to cover up this murder!" I seriously have tried many things to stop thinking of Alex and everything that happened to us that day! I even moved to Eastern Washington because I already had some old friends who flew from Mexico, Las Vegas, and California who were ready to kill these cops! However, I am trying to stay strong and give the court system one chance and to put these cops in jail for the rest of their lives. But I know they won't put these cops in jail so I went to Eastern Washington to see my grandma, grandpa, aunts, uncles, cousins, and the rest of my family and friends one last time. They have tried so hard for me to go to church in which I did many times with my grandma and I hanged out with my uncle and his family a lot. I really appreciated hanging out with them, but I had to move back to Lynden to wait and see how these cops and their associates are going to try to cover this up?

I even started smoking a pack to two packs of cigarettes a day. I am a person that never really smokes, but lately I have been smoking and drinking a lot. I even went to the emergency room once because I was going to commit suicide. No matter what I find to do, I can't stop my mind, my body, and my soul to not think of what I saw on February 28th 2011. Why can't I stop thinking of that day? Well these fucking corrupted cops who murdered my brother tell the truth or will they still try to cover it up? Am I being punished for doing something wrong a long time ago? Or is GOD testing me if I should go to Heaven? Or did that other cop shoot me and kill me and I am stuck in HELL?

I will give up whatever money I have to have my brother again! If this books makes a lot of money, I will give a lot to my brother's daughter and I will give the rest of the money to my family and friends. I don't want any fucking money, I want my brother next to me so we can live our lives until we grow old together! Is this really happening right now? Is this real? This can not be real because why would these cops shoot my brother when he was on the ground? And why did the cop tackle me off my brother while I was giving him CPR? Then the cop (cop#1) rolled my brother onto his stomach to handcuff him, then the other (cop#2) told me, "I thought he had a hammer!" Well if this really happened then we are going to have a big problem. I promise every person who reads this book….. If these cops don't go to jail, I will protest every day and do whatever it takes so they can feel my pain and also the people who are trying to cover up this murder will one day get caught on their lies!

I have realized that no matter what I buy, or spend my money on, I can never get this pain out of me. I will admit I have traveled a lot because I like to go around this world to see what this world has to offer. I like to see how other people view the world in their eyes. I like to talk to people no matter how poor they are or no matter how rich they are. Trust me I was so poor in my life growing up that my dad only made around 15,000 - 25,000 dollars year and he was trying to support five kids, a wife, himself, and then trying to help everyone around him. My dad would always try to help my uncles, aunts, cousins, brothers, sisters, and then he would try to help out my grandpa and grandma in Mexico. We were so extremely poor that we had to save money to call ourselves poor and we were even making less than some bums are making on the streets.

There was a time in my life that I would go jogging and lift weights as much as I can because my brother was in so much pain after he got hit with a baseball bat to his head. However, I would get so tired that I tried to sleep, but I can't sleep because my mind would still think about what happened to my brother. Since I was a little kid I use to play sports for about four to five hours a day with my brother. I became such a great athlete at the age of ten that no other kid could compete with me at my age. That is why I started to play with kids four to five years older than me. Even those kids weren't as good as me and a lot of those kids were angry at me because in their mind they couldn't understand on how great of an athlete I could be at a young age. And it was all because of my brother Alex. He would teach me how to play everyday and he did everything that was possible to make me a better person. I owe him my life and I will do anything to make sure he gets his justice. So if the court system won't do their job then I will have no choice to do what I need to do!

Do you know how great of an athlete I was? The main reason why I became such a great athlete was because of my speed. I was running a 40 yard dash at 4.6 seconds as a freshman. I want to tell you what I ran during some private sessions with some basketball teams and some football teams, but I don't want to brag too much.

After my freshmen year of football, I was finally convinced that I was a better athlete than everyone else and I knew I could go professional into college and who knows after that. My brother and I started to realize that I could not only help my family financially, but we could help everyone that needed help in our inner circle and then outer circle. Believe me when I say this, I was so fast at the age of ten, my average time for running the mile was at 5 minutes and 26 seconds, but back then I didn't think that was a big deal. I didn't even think, me being so great at sports was a big deal because I thought everyone could be as good as me, but soon enough I found out that I was wrong.

I was always wondering why older kids from higher grades would always pick me first for any sport when we were playing especially football, basketball, and baseball. They would always pick me first because they knew no matter what other players we had on our team, our team would always win because I was so superior to others that nobody could stop me from making the basketball in the basket, catching a football to make a touchdown, or even hitting a ball really hard in baseball, I had the athletic skills of five other kids. And I owe all those skills because my brother was teaching everyday how to become a great athlete, a great person, and eventually a great brother. Also I was a natural leader and I always had the right things to say for my teammates so not only did they believe in me, but I would say the right things so they could believe in themselves just like how Alex taught me.

One of the main reasons why I was so great at sports was because when I was in my kindergarten year, I was a really bored kid so when my brother Alex came home with his homework, I would look at it and study it. I looked at my brother's homework one day and asked him what (5x5) meant? So he told me it was like adding five, but only five times. So that was the first thing I learned from multiplication so I saw the interest of learning that and by the end of the month I knew multiplication and division. I was doing my brother's homework everyday and soon enough my brother taught me so many other things and I was addicted to learning. The reason I was addictive to learning was because my mind likes to analyze everything I see and do. Even when I try to go to sleep, my mind keeps analyzing anything I do.

When the school found out what I can do in first grade,

they started to give me assignments from kids that were in third, fifth, and seventh grade. After I took the tests, the school wanted me to skip grades every year. They informed my dad how intelligent I was and they needed my dad's permission to make me skip from first grade to third grade to my brother's class. My brother Alex didn't like that idea because he wanted me to stay in my grade level so I could be the best person in my grade level and eventually I would be superior. After a week my dad thought it would be best if I hanged out with kids my own age so I didn't get to skip grades. That got me upset so bad because I would have been able to skip two grades every year until I graduated from school.

I would have graduated school at a young age, but my dad didn't want me to go to college at a young age. Also he didn't want me to do nothing for the next couple years of my life before he thought I was old enough to go to college. He felt that I would learn more things in life if I could understand what other kids understood at my age. I thought I would always hate my dad's decision, but I realized later on that it was the best decision he could do for me because nobody can tell you how kids act when they are kids. Sure you can read about it and study it, but you can never truly understand kids unless you do it for yourself so I am proud to grow up as a kid in a way.

Even though I was a kid back then, I started to become really bored in life because I was always ahead of my class mates so I had nothing to do so I started to play all kinds of sports to keep myself not bored in life. I played everyday with my brother and older kids so I became superior in sports without even realizing it. So when I was growing up I thought my life was too easy and anything that

I wanted to do, I could do. So my whole life my brother and I were happy because we were doing something together everyday that no other kids could do. My brother Alex realized what I could do so he wanted me to try to learn as much as possible so I could do so much in my life. He knew eventually with my knowledge and skills, I would get a great career when I got older.

I was brought up by a great brother because he would always tell me, "No matter how rich or poor we are, you are never better or worst than any other person." The only thing that matters is what you do to help yourself and others. If you just care about yourself and a few other people then you are greedy and just want your way. But if you look out for other people who you don't know and try to give them something that they need some help with, well then you are someone that matters in this world." My brother has always been helping other people growing up as a kid, even though we were poor. My brother Alex would always help people and I didn't understand for a long time because we were poor. However, my brother Alex told me, "George, we all need to help each other and if one day we become millionaires... Don't tell anyone because then everyone will want your help, but if you help people without them knowing you are a millionaire and you are just doing it because it is the right thing to do than you are a good person." Ever since he told me that, I knew I would do my best to help other people. Like I said before, I didn't understand why my brother would always want to help people, but I eventually saw he not only made another person happy, but he made himself happy for helping another Human Being when they didn't have much. So naturally I wanted to do the same thing and I still want to do the same thing today!

That is why when these cops murdered my brother, they also destroyed my heart, my mind, and my soul without even realizing it. They had no clue what they did and they have no clue what I am capable of doing. I don't care who you are, if you make a mistake... You have to own up to it and do the right thing. So that is one of the reasons why I am writing this book so everyone can read it and know why I have to fight for justice no matter what the cost is.

Do you know how it feels being the best at pretty much anything you do in life when you are just a kid? My brother did anything and everything everyday to help me out because we only had each other growing up. He made me the best basketball player, football player, baseball player, and pretty much the best athlete in any sport I played. He taught me to be very intelligent in school and in life. I was the fastest kid in school and that was including being faster than most high school kids while I was in fifth grade.

I don't think I have told you that I have a sleeping disorder? Well, yes I do have a sleeping disorder since I was a baby, I can only sleep two to four hours a night. Since my mind likes to analyze everything I do, I hardly sleep because my mind is always thinking too much. That is why I am always up at night playing video games, practicing some sport, or studying life. My brother knew I couldn't sleep much in life because I had a lot to think of in my life. That was another reason I learned so much in life so fast because when I didn't sleep, my brother would give me daily assignment on how to improve myself.

Do you know how it feels to have everyone looking at you when you were just a kid? I am not saying the looks you get as a baby, but the LOOK when everyone can't believe the things you can do as such at a young age and I was better than everyone else at doing anything. Their eyes get wide open every time you walk into class or onto a basketball court because they can't believe how I was doing everything that I could do. Alex was always proud of me growing up because everyday he would hear "You are George's brother? Why is he so different or how did he become who he is? Why don't you play sports?" Everyone would stare at me and talk about me in front of my face or behind my back all the time. They would ask me sometimes on why I was so different? They asked me "How are you doing this? What goes through your mind when you are playing sports?" This is when I started to question on how other people would think because I always thought everyone could do what I could do. However, once I realized I was the only person who could do what I could do, then I started to question life. I wanted to know why people couldn't think the way I think, or do what I can do. I was obsessed to understand on how other people would think or how they reacted to a certain situation. That is why I look at the world at so many different ways, I never look at the world in one point of view, I look at the world on how other people would look at the world. Good or bad, I would consider what other people would do in my situation? That is why I am always thinking of other people's feelings first and that's another reason I want to help other people and do anything it takes for my brother and I to live a good life.

I could never sleep when I was young and I still can't sleep today. I can go days before I actually need to sleep. I usually average two to four hours of sleep on a normal night, other days I sleep maybe one or two hours. I went to the doctor to see what is wrong with me and they told me obviously that I have a sleeping disorder so they have given me medications to sleep, but it only makes me sleep no more than five hours. I usually go to sleep around 2am or up to 5am and I always wake up around 6am. My dad use to live on a farm so he would go to work at 6am every day so that is why I always waked up at 6am to see my dad walk to work.

When I knew I couldn't sleep, I would act like I was sleeping so my family or friends wouldn't think I was weird. I would just lay there with my eyes closed acting like I am sleeping, but I am just laying there thinking about life. I could always hear my brothers and my dad talking about me when I was on the couch. I slept on the couch because there wasn't enough beds for all of us and I volunteered to sleep there. My dad would always ask my brothers on how I was doing. They would always tell my dad, that everyone is talking about how smart, fast, and athletic I was. My father told them to make sure that I don't end up doing something stupid or anyone try to do something stupid to me. So my brother Alex would always be looking over me in a way to make sure I didn't get involved with drugs, alcohol, and sex. I am not going to say that I was a perfect kid because I did experiment with drugs, alcohol, and sex. However, I only smoked marijuana a couple of times in school and I drank beer for a couple of years in school.

When I was growing up as a kid, I had so many friends. I knew so many people that I stopped remembering people's names because there was too many to remember. Also Alex would always find new kids to play against me in sports so I could become a better athlete. Till this day I have too many friends so I still have a problem remembering everyone's names. I still can't believe what I gave up a long time for my brother, but I don't care because it was worth giving up everything to make sure I took care of my brother.

When I was in eighth grade, it was the year that a college scout found me. He kept on hearing from one of my brother's connection and his friends on how great of an athlete I was. When the college scout introduced himself to me, I wasn't shocked because all my life, Alex told me that I was very gifted and one day I will become very wealthy because of my superior skills. He explained to my brother and I by the time I graduated from high school that a lot of professional sports are going to be selecting high school players instead of college players because they want younger players to make them money faster and longer. Even though the NBA has changed their rules now and the NFL always want their players out of college. Well after I graduated high school, I noticed that a lot of high school stars did get selected to be professional athletes right away. The same year I graduated high school was when I saw a lot of team's select high school players in the NBA Lottery. I told the college scout that the only thing that made me happy growing up was hanging out with my brother because he did anything to make sure I had anything that I wanted in life.

Playing sports everyday just made me stop thinking of the world for a second and even though it felt great playing in that sport's world, I knew it couldn't be with me for eternity. Why do you think all the greatest athletes come out of retirement? They come out of retirement because nothing in the world makes them happy to their FULL

POTENTIAL. Trust me, when I use to be on a basketball court or football field, I felt like I was on a natural high that made me feel so great. However, every time I stepped of the court or football field, all I had was my brother. I knew one day with my skills, I could repay back my brother by achieving our goal in life......

When the college scout came to me, he taught me something I would never forget in my life. He told me that I should never show my true potential until it was the right time. He told me that because he says, "Once someone knows how far your skills can go, they will do anything to reach farther to beat you." He told me to remember one thing, "Expect the Unexpected." Also he wanted me to hold back so no other school knew much about me and he wanted me to go to his college. That was perfect advice because you can never expect something from me, but you would expect something unexpected. So I started to hold back no matter what it was, with school grades, my speed in running, my athletic skills, and I started to not show my full potential anymore.

Every time I started to play basketball against really great athletes I only played good enough to beat them, I never played too great to embarrass them because then they would know how great I was. However, one day when I was a freshman, the best AAU players from another city challenged me to play against them. These kids were great players, the previous year most of them were starting varsity players for a very good school and they were in the top five in state the previous year. Well I didn't want to beat them and embarrass them so I chose some not so good players to play with me.

Once we started to play against these players, my

brother told me to hold back and they took no time to start humiliating us really bad. It got me a little ticked off because they kept on taunting me and they kept on trying to tell me that I was only a great player against my own age so then I decided to play a lot harder. The score was 28 to 9 and we were playing to 50 points. They were laughing at us so bad because my teammates really didn't know how to dribble or even pass the ball that well. So I started playing offensively by myself against five of the best players in our county. I told my teammates to play defensively only and in a zone area so no player can shoot a lay in or an easy shot. Then I eventually started to play to my full potential and came back to win by 52 to 42. They got so pissed off because they heard how great I was, but they never believed I was that superior. They got so pissed off that one of the players told me, "We are never going to play with you again." After that day, a lot of people didn't want to play with me anymore, but my brother would just laugh and tell me, "You have a crazy gift so don't screw this up."

In school, I use to get nothing but A's in class my whole life. I only missed four days of school since kindergarten to my sixth grade. That was for many reasons because I had nothing to do at home besides study and hang out with my brother. Also I went to school as much as I could because since my family was so poor I could go to school and eat for free. Also I got a lot of awards saying how many days I never missed school and for how great of an athlete I was. The other reason I went to school every day was because my brother didn't want me to be hanging out with our family alone. I love and respect my dad's other family, but Alex was the only person who I trusted in life because of all the things we went through together so I tried to hang out with him all the time.

Like I said before I would get nothing but A's all my life but since my college scout told me not to show my full potential anymore. I started to get some B's, C's, and some A's. Everyone I knew always thought they knew how smart I was, but they never knew how smart I really was. Even after I went to college, I knew I could get nothing but A's, but I ended up getting a crappy G.P.A so people didn't realize my true potential. Also, grades don't define a person, only the person who goes after their dreams and achieve their goals defines that person. A lot of people are wrong about me because when I was going to college full time, I had a full time job working from 11pm until 7am five days a week and I went to college all year round from 8am until around 4pm. I had morning and afternoon classes because I took 19 to 27 credits every semester. I didn't even take the summers off because I wanted to graduate as soon as possible so I could take care of my brother and I graduated college in less than three years. I also worked out at the gym four days a week and I ran five miles every other day. So you are thinking when did I sleep, well since I hardly slept growing up, it was pretty easy not to sleep and to do all that stuff. All I heard when I was in college, was..... I was crazy for doing all those things. I haven't even told you my party life when I was going through college.

When I didn't show my true potential and I didn't do something right, people would always try to help me out. I am not saying I am perfect because I am not, but it's funny when people try to help me out because I am very educated. You are probably thinking I lied a lot in my life, but not really. I am not perfect and I did some horrible things growing up, but what I saw on February 28th 2011 was the worst thing in the world for my brother and I. So I will do anything that is possible for the truth to come out. DO YOU UNDERSTAND WHY THIS BOOK IS CALLED "Cops murdered my brother so what do I do now?" My brother sacrificed his life so I could have a good life with him and now I am willing to sacrifice my life again so we both can live in peace.

I am praying for my brother everyday because I don't know where he is at and I want to make sure he knows I am still here no matter what happens. This is another reason why I wrote this book because I would like a prayer from each person who reads this book to pray for my brother to be in a good place. I don't care if you are religious or not, I just would like a prayer so God can know that wherever my brother is at, he is truly missed and he should be happy wherever he is at. All I want is one prayer, asking the lord to help my brother out and our family out through this horrible tragedy. I know the lord sees our pain, feels our pain, sees our tears, and sees our blood. If I can get that prayer from each person who reads this book then I know the Lord will help my brother out and to make sure he doesn't suffer anymore. Because to be honest with you, I don't care what happens to me, all I want is for everyone to live a good life so they don't end up with the pain that I am going through. I don't want anyone to feel what I am going through, I am tired of seeing the tears of people, I am tired of all the terrible things that people go through, I am tired of all the evilness that happens to people in this world. So I hope you understand that we need to help each other out no matter what the situation is.

Dear Reader,

Thank you for reading this book and I hope you realize

that there is still good people in this world that want to help each other out.

Thank you Lord for everything that you have given me, please Lord help the people who need it the most. Help the children who go through problems everyday. Help the people who don't have the capabilities to do things that other people have everyday. Every good person needs your help, even the people who might not be so innocent still need your help to live a better life. We can all change to become human beings who are here to help each other out. All we need is a little help from you, please Lord bless us with your hand once again. Thank you Lord

Who was my Alex and I?

I have been trying to explain to you who my brother and I was, but there is so much that you need to know. My brother was born in August of 1980 and I was born in December of 1982. We were not greedy people because honestly we hated money. We got our first job at the age of seven and nine years old, we would mow lawns and with our first paycheck we got twenty dollars. After we got our check we went to the store and bought some candy then ran home and sat on our couch. We started to watch television, then we saw a commercial to the kids who lived with hardly any food or water in Africa. After we saw that commercial, my brother told me that we should send some money to the kids in Africa. I asked him why and he said, "Even though we don't have much, these kids don't have anything and they don't have the opportunities as we do and we should help out other people who need it the most."

I didn't really understand during the time, but I did become a better person because of that situation. We didn't care that our family was poor too and that we were barely surviving in America, but the only thing he was thinking about was how we could make another dollar for the kids in Africa. I really wish I was making this up so you could think my brother was this awesome kid growing up. However, my brother really did feel sorry for the kids in Africa and any other person who didn't have the opportunities that we had. Our step-mom called the people on the commercial because we weren't 18 years old and they gave us instructions on how we were going to send the money.

You also need to know that my brother and I grew up in a very weird way. When our mom died when my brother was four and I was two years old, my dad had to work all day and night to support my two brothers and I. He had a very hard labor job that paid minimum wage, but it was the only job that he could do. Since he had to work so much, he put my two brothers in charge of the house and my two brothers were suppose to teach me how to do things in life. However, my brother Alex was the only person who talked to me and taught me things because my oldest brother didn't like living with us and moved to Eastern Washington. So my brother Alex was more than my brother growing up, he was my best friend, and like a father to me.

When my dad did come home from work around 9PM, my brother and I would be in our rooms sleeping or on the couch, but I wouldn't be sleeping. I would have my eyes closed and I would just analyze the things I do in life until I fell asleep. Since my dad worked five to seven days a week, he hardly ever saw me. So, whenever he did see me, he would always say, "How are you doing and how are you doing in school?" I would always respond by saying, "I am ok." Then he would say, "Well try your hardest in school so you can get a good job." My dad seriously never talked to me growing up and we would go months and months without talking to each other. I even started to count the words my dad would say to me and the total amount was 3148 words. That was from when I was in first grade until I graduated high school! If you ever meet me, you will learn quickly that I can barely speak Spanish because since my dad or family members hardly spoke to me, I never learned Spanish properly so Alex taught me English and everything else besides Spanish.

After I turned turned seven years old, my dad realized that he couldn't raise two kids by himself so he took us to California one day and he dropped us off for a week at our aunt's house. Then my dad came to pick us up a week later with our new step-mother. Yes, this is very true. My dad went to Mexico and got married and came back within a week. However, when we got back home, our step-mother just cooked us food and she hardly spoke to me as well. My dad started a new family with his new wife and Alex and I were in our room just living our lives together with hardly any help from my dad.

Ever since we were kids, my brother my brother tried his best to be a good person. So every time I saw a kid that needed help in school or in the real world, I would go out of my way to help them out. When I was in school from first grade to fourth grade, some times my teacher would even let me teach class some days because kids will learn a lot of things easier when they see another kid doing what they are trying to learn. When I was a kid, the best thing I liked to do was to teach other kids how to play sports a lot better because I was doing what my brother did for me. I always selected the worst players to be on my team because I wanted the other kids to have fun by learning how to play better and to be on the winning team. However, when I completed all my homework for the week my teachers would always let me play outside with my brother when he had his recess and lunch. Most of the times I would practice my basketball skills, football skills, baseball skills, or I would even just run a couple miles with my brother telling me what I could do better. The school didn't know what to do with me since I wasn't able to skip grades and I didn't have much to learn anymore so they let the P.E. teacher be my coach a couple days of the week and he taught me a lot too. Some times I was even taken to my brother's class to play with the older kids and do my homework with him.

I would even help teenagers and even adults when I was growing up. I had so many kids that would come up to me all the time and they would always want me to teach them certain things in school or they would call my house. I even got calls from other student's parents and they would want to know the answers on the questions they couldn't figure out for their kids. Then I was getting so many calls at one point that my dad had to change our phone number and kept our number private. Nobody could look up our phone number and the school didn't get our new number either, but they got the number to my dad's work site. We kept our phone number very private and we kept it very private until I graduated high school.

Playing with older kids was one of the reasons why I became a great athlete and a great person in life. My brother was teaching me what each basketball player position should do. Once I knew each position then I would study on what their weaknesses and strengths should be. I started to understand if I could dribble the ball with two hands then I could become a greater player. I would practice dribbling for an hour every day with my brother; either at school or at the park. Within eight months, I became a better dribbler than the starting point guard for all the AAU teams that I played with or against. Also during this time, I would practice every day with my brother or with other people on how to steal the ball. My brother taught me that I should count in my head and look at the ball on how the other player is dribbling the ball. Once I figured out their dribbling patterns, I would reach out with my hand to steal the ball. My brother would be very aggressive with me by pushing, shoving, or even elbowing me so I could learn how to play rough and not get mad.

After I learned how to dribble and steal the ball phenomenal, I started to practice on shooting the ball. Since, I was a lot smaller than the other kids I had to use my speed to shoot the ball and lay the ball in. I also had great jumping skills so I would always practice to jump towards the hoop from one side and then make the shot from the other side of the hoop. My brother was a lot taller than me so his height really helped me to shoot the ball certain ways so my shot wasn't blocked. I learned how to spin the ball off the backboard so it helped me make a lot of my shots. I would shoot a lot of three pointers because I knew I would become a point guard so after a long time of practicing, I learned how to make three pointers consistently. Also I haven't mentioned that my coach was an ex-starting point guard in college so I learned a lot from him. (Thank you Josh) He taught me so many little tricks on how to trick my opponent on where I was going to dribble the ball or when I was going to shoot the ball. My coach even showed me video tapes of professional basketball players and how they played. He was showing me what professional shooting point guards do in the NBA so it helped my skills a lot by seeing those tapes.

Alex taught me so many things because he saw so much potential in me and he especially made me practice defense more than my offensive skills. The reason he taught me defense more was he believed and I believe too, that if I can be a better defensive player than an offensive player than I have more of a chance to win a game. If I was able to steal the ball or make the other opponent try to make a hard shot than I would have a chance to win the game a lot more. (That is why you hear the quote, Defense wins championships.) Also the reason I was taught to be a great defense of player was because it made me become a better offensive player. If I knew what a great defensive of player is trying to do when I have the ball than I can use that information to my advantage.

I was taught how to play football, baseball, and how to run a lot better as well. When it was the days to play football, Alex was teaching me to be a wide receiver. So I would be practicing running certain routes and catching the ball. He also showed me on how to fake my opponent on where I was going to run my route so I could get open to catch the ball. Then after months of learning how to catch the ball with two hands, Alex started making me start only using one hand so I could catch the ball. It took me a long time to learn to catch the football with one hand properly, but after months and months of intense training, I became really great on catching the football with one hand.

Alex started to realize that I couldn't just be a wide receiver so he started to train me to become a punt returner and a kick off returner. He showed me that I needed to pick a certain place to run before the ball is kicked to me. Then he told me that I shouldn't worry about the first person I see because with my speed and skills I have, I can easily pass him so I should only worry about the next person who I think will tackle me. This was so true because after learning to be a great receiver, I knew I could get away from my first opponent, but it was the second person who I should be worry about. So after months and months of practicing, I learned many skills on how to avoid my opponents. I was so great as a returner that I wasn't allowed to return the ball anymore in flag football because I would always run by everyone and score a touchdown. Also Alex taught me on where the ball should be in my hands so whenever I got hit, the ball would be secured and it wouldn't pop out of my hands.

Alex taught me how to be a corner back on defense so I could learn what the defense players are thinking when I am a wide receiver trying to catch the ball. He taught me how the corner will run with me and where the corner hands will be when he is trying to cover me. After learning how to catch the ball so well with one hand, it helped me a lot playing defense and making interceptions with one hand. My skills were getting so superior that everyone around me started to always talk about me. Also Alex was getting video tapes from my old coach on how professional athletes in the NFL and how they practiced and played in the NFL.

I only practiced playing baseball once a week because Alex wanted me to concentrate more on football and basketball. Also it was because I could only do so much in baseball. Alex was given 50 baseballs from my old coach and he would pitch to me so I could practice my swinging skills. He showed me that I should observe the pitcher on how he pitches because I could learn what kind of pitch he will pitch me by his body motion. After learning how to swing the ball, I decided that I would be a center fielder for defense in baseball. Alex showed me on how to run towards the ball when it is hit to me and how to catch the ball. Then he showed me how to throw the ball towards second base, third base, and to home plate. After I was done learning those skills, I was taught how to steal bases. I really liked stealing bases. He showed me exactly where to stand at my base and to observe the pitcher properly so I could get a good jump start. However, with my speed skills as a kid, I was able to steal bases all the time. Alex didn't show me tapes of any professional athletes in the MLB because he didn't really want to me learn that much of baseball.

I was taught how to become a better runner as well. Alex taught me how to breathe when I am running and how my hands should move when I was running. We set goals for running a mile and running two miles. When I first ran my first mile, I ran it in six minutes and thirty-three seconds. Like I said before, I was a natural runner and a fast kid. That first mile was when I was in first grade! However, Alex didn't want to push me too hard in running long distance so he mostly taught me how to sprint a lot faster.

Alex had me practice my basketball skills on Monday and Tuesday. He would make me practice my football skills on Wednesday and Thursdays. I would only practice my baseball skills on Fridays because that was the day the other kids would play baseball so I would play with them. I would run three to five miles on Monday, Wednesday, and on Friday. On Saturday and Sundays, I would always go to the park and either play basketball or football with Alex and other kids. I lived only a half mile away from the park so I got to play against a lot older kids when I was growing up. As you can tell, I was learning how to play sports like a rich family would teach their child to play. Rich families pay for personal coaches and make their child practice everyday so they can become a great athlete. However, I wasn't rich, but since I had nothing else to do in school, I got to play and learn to play sports everyday for free and spend all my time with my brother.

I can still remember the days I would run to school in the morning so I could get there early so I could play basketball or football in the morning. I was always selected to be a captain for the team so I could pick a fair team to play with. Those were some great days because my mind wouldn't think of anything else when I was playing basketball, football, or baseball. All I could think of was to how to make the basketball in the basket or catching the football to score the touchdown. I was in a complete different world when I was playing sports, but when I didn't play any sports, my mind would wonder off.

My school also made me go see the counselor once a week after they found out how intelligent I was. I told my counselor how my life was going and nothing challenged me except for Alex. I also told my counselor that I loved playing sports because it would calm me down and I wouldn't think of things at my house, in life, or at school. So when the counselor heard everything I had to say, the school decided to let me play all the different sports all the time. They knew since my dad wasn't going to let me skip grades, they could at least try to let me have fun at school instead of being bored with life. When I got to talk to the counselor once a week, I learned so many other things than no other kids would learn. However, I will not let you know what she taught me because I am not going to let you know everything about me.

One day when I was eight years old, a friend, my two brothers, and I were walking to a store and then we heard gun shots. We saw a car pass us and some guy was yelling some racist slurs and shooting at us. It happened so fast, but at the same time it seemed like everything was in slow motion because I can still remember the guy's face and you can see the machine gun in his hand pointing out of his car window. The guy was a racist and I didn't hear what he said, but my brother told my dad and I later on that he was yelling, "You fucking beaners, go to hell." The next day, the car was burnt in the woods and the police couldn't find out who owned the vehicle.

After that happened, my dad took my brother and I to our pastor's sons gym. Our pastor had a boxing gym so he taught us how to be a boxer every Saturday morning. Learning how to fight was a good thing for me because I learned how to protect myself. However, my brother got into a lot of fights growing up because he liked to beat people who were racist and always calling him names. However, he wouldn't start a fight, he would only protect himself and protect me.

Do you understand how great of a player I was yet? I practiced everyday from when I was in first grade until I moved to Lynden when I was in fifth grade. I would not only practice at school for an hour or two, but I would practice at home or at the park for another couple of hours every day with Alex. If I wasn't practicing with other kids, I was practicing by myself and my brother throughout my entire childhood. I knew I was a great player, but once I moved to the other city and the other school, I wanted to change.

My dad decided to move right next to his job so that meant we had to move to a different school when I was in fifth grade. Before I moved, I talked to my counselor a couple times and I told her that I didn't want to be "The Guy" everyone keeps on talking about. I didn't want to be famous anymore and I didn't want everyone to treat me different. I just wanted to be a normal kid and I wanted to try to live a "Normal life." So we concluded that once I moved to my new school and once I started going to class that I wouldn't try so hard anymore. You have to understand that when I was going to school at Jester, everyone in the town knew who I was. I seriously would have people come up to me at the park, store, or on the sidewalk and ask me, "Are you George Martinez?" Everyone would always look at me and talk about me. I was just tired of being treated different and I just wanted to be like the other kids in my school so when I moved, I promised myself that I wouldn't show my full potential anymore. Also my counselor talked to the principal and he told me that they wouldn't mention anything about me when my paper work was transferred to the new school.

My dad was tired of all the attention our family was getting too so that was another reason we moved. My dad moved us one week after I started fifth grade and honestly it was hard moving away because I knew I wasn't going to be able to see my best friend every day anymore. We moved outside of the city instead of being inside the city again, I knew everything around me would be a lot quieter. Also the first day we moved to our new mobile home, I found out that we were neighbors with my dad's boss. My dad or none of my family members didn't tell me that my dad's boss had a full basketball court. He also made the court to be a tennis court so I learned how to play tennis.

On the first day we moved, my family left me alone at the house and my dad's boss came over on his four wheeler. He came to my door and said, "You must be George, your dad told me that you are really smart and really good at sports. You are welcome to come over to my house any time and play basketball or play any time that you want." I thanked him for his offer and I also told him that I usually practice every day in the morning and at night. He told me that he didn't mind because he gets up to work from 5:30 AM and he doesn't go to sleep until 10 PM. Also he had lights for his basketball and tennis court! After I found out about his basketball court and I was allowed to play whenever I wanted, I knew it was destiny for me to keep on practicing.

After we got done moving, I went to school and started my new life. My first day of school didn't turn out the way I wanted it to go. The reason it didn't turn out to be a good day was because our first assignment that was handed to the class was to do 100 multiple and division problems. Also the assignment was a time evaluation to determine what kids were good at math and what kids needed help in math. So when my teacher told the class to start our assignment, I quickly answered all the questions within two minutes, I stood up because we were told to stand up after we were done with all the problems. So after I stood up, my teacher thought that I needed to use the restroom or had a question so he said, "George, you need to sit down and try to finish all the problems that you can do." However, I told him that I was finished so I walked towards him and handed him the paper. So after I turned around, I saw a lot of kids staring at me and some thought I was joking because their face had an expression of, "laughter and one said, yeah right," but some other kids had a face like, "Is he serious?"

My teacher saw that I did answer all the problems, but he thought that they couldn't be all right so he told me to sit down until he called my name. I sat down at my chair and then I was seeing my teacher trying to find any incorrect answers on my paper, but after he went through every problem and he couldn't find an incorrect answer, he went over the paper again. He was holding his red pen along my paper the entire time and then he scratched his head with confusion three times. After he went over the paper twice, he called my name so I went over to his desk. He said, "How did you do all of these problems so fast?" I just told him that I was really good in math. So when we had a break to go to recess, he took out another piece of paper out of his desk and he told me that I should do all of the 100 problems sitting at his desk so he could observe me doing the problems. So again I quickly answered all the questions again and he said, "Wow, who taught you math?" I told him that my brother taught me a lot of things so I am pretty good at math.

The only time I did play sports in my sixth grade year was at my dad's boss's house. My dad's boss didn't realize how dedicated I was playing basketball, playing tennis, and football. During my fifth and sixth grade year in school, I would go to Chuck's house everyday. Chuck is my dad's boss's name. My brother and I would go to his house before I had to go to school and we would go to his house after I got out of school every day. Some days he would finish early and he would come out and play with us. He figured out that I was extremely athletic because he played basketball and baseball all of his life, but he couldn't guard me. I was able to steal the ball from him if he tried to make a lay up. Also he was 6' 6" and he was the starting forward for his high school team three years in a row. He won state championship in basketball in his senior year and I could tell that he was a good basketball player, but I was too fast, too good of a dribbler, and I had too many good shots that he couldn't block. He was very impressed with my skills and he even had some of his friends come over to play against me or to be on his team.

During the time I was always playing sports mainly by myself, while my brother Alex would be helping my dad working in the raspberry fields to make money. And during the times when I wasn't practicing or playing sports, I would be helping my dad working in the raspberry fields too. It didn't matter if the weather was windy, rainy, snowy, muddy, or really sunny because we had to work no matter what to make a buck. We know how hard it is to make a buck so we did what was necessary to make a living.

I was the best player in my school and I wasn't trying my hardest. One day when I was running home after practice, a police officer parked in front of me and stopped me. The officer got out of his car and immediately arrested me (when I say the police officer arrested me, I mean he put handcuffs on me to question me). Apparently there was a house burglary near by and since he saw a Hispanic male running, he figured I was the person who committed the crime. After 30 minutes talking to the police officer and telling him that I just left football practice, we finally got a hold of my dad at home so my dad and my brother came to pick me up. At first the police officer didn't think I was on the football team and didn't think I was the best player because I kept on telling the officer, "I am on the football team and I am also the best player." However, the cops said, "Sure you are and all Mexicans don't do crimes." This pissed me off, but once the cop got a call from another cop that they caught the "Caucasian male" who committed the crime, the cop finally let me go when my dad and brother came to pick me up.

Ever since I was arrested that day, my brother or my dad would come to pick me up after practice or games. One day after my brother picked me up from a football game in my 7th grade year, a police officer pulled my brother over because he claimed my brother was speeding. However, we didn't speed or do illegal things back then because we don't have the money to pay for tickets or to go to court. So when the police officer came to the driver side window, he took a big smell into our car and said, "I smell marijuana so who is carrying the marijuana?" And I was completely shocked because during that time, my brother and I wasn't doing illegal drugs. So we just laughed and told the officer that none of us do any kind of drugs. So he wanted to search our car and by that time another police officer came onto the scene. They searched the entire car for over an hour because they couldn't find anything. They handcuffed my brother and I, and we were standing right next to the police car for over an hour. Then one officer came to me and the other officer took my brother to the other side of the car.

The cop said to me, "We know you guys have drugs in the car, but it's best that you tell us where the drugs are at. If you tell us where the drugs are at, then we can work something out that you won't get much in trouble, but if we keep looking and find the drugs then both of you guys are going to go to jail." I just laughed at the cop and told him that we don't do drugs and to keep searching the car. When the cops stopped questioning us, my brother and I were standing right next to each other again. My brother told me what the cop told him and it was the exactly the same thing he told me. We both just started laughing again because the cops thought we did drugs and they couldn't find any drugs. Well, when one of the officers saw us laughing together and they couldn't find anything, so one officer came towards my brother and punched him in the stomach. My brother went down on his knees and I yelled, "What the fuck man, why the fuck did you do that?" The officer just said, "Well what's so funny? We know you guys do drugs!" So after another half hour of searching the car, the cops still couldn't find anything so they took the handcuffs off us and left. We got one of the officer's license plates.

The next day we went to the police station and reported that we got searched and my brother got hit by one of the officers. We showed them the license plate number and they told us there would be an investigation. However, we didn't hear nothing for a month so when my brother and I went back to the police station to see what's going on with the investigation, the supervisor told us that it was our word against two police officer's word and they said, "The police officer pulled us over for speeding and one of the officer's smelled marijuana, but after searching the vehicle they couldn't find drugs so they let us go." What the fuck? So my brother and I left.... And my brother told me, "Don't worry bro, this is how life is so we have to be better than them and just let it go." I am not saying my brother was perfect growing up and I am not saying I was perfect growing up, but when we keep on having police harass us and accuse us of illegal things, there isn't much a Mexican or a minority can do. So I just kept on focusing on playing sports and being the best I can be.

After having a great football season as a freshmen, I had to start practicing to play basketball. On my second day of basketball practice some kids ran into the gym and said, "George, George! Something happened to your brother a few blocks away from school, you have to come!" So I ran as fast as I could to the spot where they told me where my brother was and by the time I got there, he was laying on the ground with a lot of blood around him. My brother couldn't move or talk so when the ambulance got there, they rushed him to the hospital. You could tell he was really injured because his whole side of his face was covered in blood and there was about 30 students around the ambulance and the spot where my brother was hit. Apparently some kids jumped out of truck when my brother was walking with his friends and one kid hit my brother in the back of the head with a baseball bat and then the kids took off. So I got a ride to my house and told my family on what happened so we all went to the hospital right away.

When I got to the hospital there was about 20 relatives there and over 50 students and teachers at the hospital. The cops were there and they were getting statements from some of the students who saw the crime and they told us that they got the people arrested on who hurt my brother. I didn't speak to anyone during this time, but a lot of people kept on saying something to me, but I mentally blocked everyone from my mind. The doctors wouldn't let anyone to see my brother because he was in surgery and they didn't know what would happen to him. I didn't want to stay in the hospital so I asked one of my teachers if he could take me to the mall so I can stop thinking of what was going on so he did. When we were walking around the mall, we went inside the Footlocker store and my teacher told me, "Do you have any shoes for basketball season yet?" I said, "I am just using the same shoes I use every year." (We didn't have money to buy new shoes every year.) Then he picked up some new Michael Jordan shoes and asked my size. I told him size 9.5, but then I told him I was going to the restroom.

I went into the restroom and put water all over my face and I kept on looking at the mirror thinking, "What the hell is going on? Is this really happening?" When I came out of the restroom, I told my teacher I wanted to go back to the hospital. He agreed and then he handed me a bag. I opened the bag and saw it was the new Michael Jordan shoes (Michael Jordan version 13) and I told him that he shouldn't have done that. He told me that his nephew admires me at school and that everyone wishes they were like me and he knew our family was poor and that he wanted to help me out. (I still have those shoes in my bank vault) I thanked him and when we got to the hospital I saw everyone crying or not talking or with their heads down

My brother was out of surgery, but he was in his room. The doctor told my dad that my brother was severely hurt and we just have to wait and see what happens. He didn't want to say my brother would recover or not because he lost a lot of blood and he was severely hurt. So we had to wait and pray for the best.

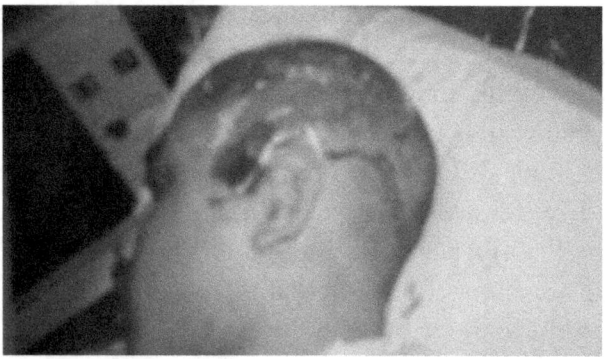

This is my brother after he was hit with a baseball bat

After my brother was hit with the baseball bat to the back of the head, he couldn't talk for two days. After he finally woke up, after days and days of sleeping, I went into his room and he didn't recognize who I was. I was in complete shock and I had to talk to him for two weeks so he can start remembering me. He told me that he just remembered walking and then falling on the ground. I told my brother that I wanted to hurt that guy, but he convinced me it wouldn't be worth it and to let the court do their job. However, that kid only got a few months of juvenile time. That was total bull shit and if that person wasn't white and if he was a Mexican or an African American that hit a Caucasian with a bat, we would go to jail for attempted murder!

The reason that guy hit my brother with the baseball bat, was that guy got beat up from my brother Alex. He was calling Alex some racist remarks and when he picked a fight with Alex, Alex defended himself and beat up the guy. However, since that guy was so upset Alex beat him up in front of his friends, he decided to leave and come back with a bat. He jumped out of the truck while my brother was walking towards the store and my brother didn't see the kid and the kid hit my brother in the side of the head. Also after the Police Officer #3 fell down and hit his head, well....... If he got hit with a hammer like when my brother got hit by a baseball bat, he wouldn't be telling everyone, "I am ok, I am ok." Also he wouldn't be let out of the hospital within 24 hours!

I stopped playing sports and started working with my dad in the raspberry fields more to support the family and to take care of Alex. I tried playing football my junior year of High School, but my heart wasn't into sports anymore, my heart was only in taking care of my brother. However, since my brother got hit in the head, his would complain a lot because his head hurt. He couldn't think normal all the time so he would smoke marijuana and drink alcohol to stop the pain. He started doing other drugs to get rid of the pain because vicodin and other medicine wouldn't help his head from not hurting. So my brother was going in and out of jail because of his drug problems. I tried my best to stop him from doing drugs, but it was really hard to make him stop using drugs. He would stop doing drugs on and off when I was around, but if I wasn't around he would start doing drugs again. When my brother went to jail and was given a few years of jail time, I took that opportunity to go to college so when he got out of jail, I would have a good job to take care of him.

You are probably wondering when I will start talking about Alex's life more? Well, Alex was George and George was Alex! Don't you get it yet? I was Alex and Alex was me! When he was going through pain that's when I was feeling pain! When I was feeling pain, he was feeling pain! When I was playing sports, Alex was the person everyone was admiring. When I was getting good grades, Alex was the one who was getting good grades! So when these fucking stupid mother fucking cops killed Alex, well that's when they killed me! That's when they killed us! Do you get it yet? Do you understand why I wrote this book yet? Well, they made a huge mistake and I am going to try to fix it!

I gave up my college career for Alex! I gave up my life for Alex because he gave up his life so I can have a better life! Do you understand what I am doing yet? If not, well let me tell you.... I am giving up my life again so this entire world understand that these cops fucked up! The way these cops fucked up is by.... Our taxes pay for the police to protect us.... But what happens when the police get greedy and try to control us? What happens when your taxes pays for the government to protect us, but they aren't protecting us anymore, they are just protecting themselves! They are doing whatever it takes to help each other out, but when they screw up, they try to pay the family or people off? They don't care about us or the rest of the country! They only care about themselves! Why do you think they paid off the banks out of debt? We were so much in debt because all the big businesses scammed everyone so what did the government do? They gave them a bailout off your tax money! That is like giving a car thief that got caught millions of dollars because he didn't know how to steal properly!

So like I said before!..... Who will be murdered next? And remember your voice doesn't mean shit because they are living in their mansions and living off our tax money. They say, they are trying to help us out, but I will admit some people are, but most of them just care about themselves. Why is it, that they will spend millions of dollars investigating sexual behavior when the mayor, governor, or president does something wrong? But they won't spend millions of dollars on investigating 9/11 or spend millions of dollars on how they screwed up on going to war on Iraq? Don't you guys understand that your tax money is for them to work for you and not the other way around? They shouldn't be telling us on what's best for us, why do you think there is a America? It's because those people came to this land to be free and not be controlled by their country. I love the United States, but are we really free or are we slowly being controlled?

Aren't we all human beings? Don't our voice matter? I can go rob a bank and get many years in jail. Or, I can start up a bank and then get in debt millions of dollars and then I can get bailed out by the United States Citizens taxes and then pay my employees millions of dollars for bonuses! Don't you people understand that your tax money was given to the banks that made our country in debt, but instead of punishing them, we gave them more money so they could start over? Does that really make sense? I know people are going to say that we needed to bail them out because the entire country was going to collapse if we didn't so does that mean every criminal in jail should be released and given a million dollars each? Who are the bigger and worst criminals? The people who are in jail for robbery, the people who are in jail for violence, the people who do illegal drugs or the people who aren't in jail in which got this country in debt?

Double life

I started to play poker in the year 2003 and I became addicted to playing because I was great at playing poker and I loved playing poker! Since I knew my brother was going to get out of jail soon when I was in college, I knew I needed a job to make a lot of money, but I couldn't work too many hours because I would need to spend a lot of hours to take care of my brother. So I thought about robbing banks because I could find the best way to rob banks without getting caught. But I knew if I robbed banks than I would ruin a person's mind because he or she would be afraid to go to work if someone threatened them for money. I could sell drugs and make millions of dollars after a few years, but I knew I would kill a lot of people and ruin a lot of people lives by selling drugs. So I decided to play poker and I made a lot money off it.

I knew if I got a career job with my degrees and my knowledge, I would have to work long hours to make enough money to support my brother and help out a lot of family members and friends. Playing poker was really easy for me to do because it was about math and reading your opponent. I did this all my life and this is how I became a great poker player. First, I would play against friends, but you didn't make much money off friends or at house poker nights. (I made about 500-1200 dollars a month off friends and poker games at people's houses. Then I went to play in the casinos to play, but again I wasn't make that much money. (I made around 100-5,000 dollars a month) And some months I would lose money) Also when you are at a casino, you lose money by buying drinks and food because you are playing for many hours. So then I started to play poker on-line and then ....

I started to make a lot of money playing poker on-line! When you play poker on-line, you can play in as many as games at once, while if you play at a house or at a Casino, then you only play one game at a time. However, when you play at home on-line, you can play so many different games at one time and make more money. Also you can play at home at any time of the day because there are always people playing 24/7! There are so many different type of poker games you can play on-line and you can play for a few cents at a time or up to hundreds of thousands of dollars at a time. You can play poker tournaments in which you can pay $10 dollars to enter and then win thousands of dollars if you win the tournament.

I am not going to say how much I have won because I don't want anyone to know how much money I have. However, I have placed in some poker tournaments in which I made over $150,000 each. I also made a lot of money playing against other people on-line in private poker table games. So once I was making a lot of money.... That is when I started to live a double life. I didn't want to tell anyone how rich I was because I wanted to take care of my brother and help people out without them knowing I was wealthy. And this is how I kept my double life a secret until right now.

1. Don't become a drug addict or a alcoholic! (The number one reason why a criminal gets caught doing illegal things is because they have a drug or alcohol problem. When someone has a drug or alcohol problem, they slip up or get careless when they do illegal things and they eventually get caught.

2. Don't tell anyone on what you do or how much money you have! (The second reason why a criminal gets

caught is because he tells a girlfriend/wife, family members, or friends on what he is doing. If one day he gets his girlfriend/wife, family members, or a friend upset then one of those people will tell the police on what illegal things that person is doing.

3. Don't get greedy! (The third reason why a criminal gets caught is because he gets greedy. The person starts buying a nice car, a big house, luxury items, and starts showing off all the things he has and attracts too much attention. So I carefully didn't become that greedy person to a certain degree.)

4. Buy a house or a nice car in a different state. (Don't have luxury items near where you live and where people know you from.)

5. Get a fake name and a fake I.D. (You can get a "Real" fake license with the right amount of money.)

6. Find a lawyer that will help you "Clean your money. (You can go to 10 different criminal defense lawyers with $10,000 dollars cash and one out of ten lawyers will tell you how to "Clean your money.")

7. Never spend your money on anything when using your real name. (Don't pay a electric bill, a cell phone bill, rent, food, or anything when using your real name. I never used my poker money on my real name even though I am in debt with my real name.)

8. Buy a car in another person's name. (I would put another person's name on all my cars vehicle registration.)

9. You must have a real job in your real name. (No matter what kind of job, even if you have a minimum wage job, you must have a job so people aren't suspicious that

you are paying your bills and having nice things without a job.)

10. Don't always go out with family and friends. (From time to time, when people invite you to go out, just say, "I am sorry, but I am broke right now so I can't go out. That way people will think you don't always have money to spend.)

11. Keep buying pre-paid cell phones and change your number every six months. (Always buy pre-paid cell phones in cash and always buy them in different stores. Just incase the cops or I.R.S are suspicious of what you do, then they won't be able to detect on the places you travel if you keep the same phone and phone number all the time. Remember, cops can detect where you are at by the cell phone towers.)

12. Buy a used car every six months to a year. (Only buy used cars with your real name that you can afford. Just incase you are being watched or being bugged then switch cars. When you switch cars, the police have to get a new warrant to put a tracking device in your car.)

13. Don't use store cards for discounts. (The store cards for discounts keep records on how much you spend on them so if you use a store card, the I.R.S can investigate those store cards.)

14. Always pay in Cash! (You should always pay for stuff in cash unless you get prepaid VISA cards.)

15. Don't wear flashy clothes or jewelry. (Like I said before, don't show off and attract attention!)

16. Don't do anything illegal when you are depress or need the money for desperation. (A lot of people get really careless when they "Really need the money" so their mind

isn't thinking clearly and that is when they do a lot of mistakes.)

17. Don't tell anyone and I seriously mean don't tell anyone what you are doing. (I never told anyone what I have been doing because I wanted to help people and I like to live a private life. Also the other reason I never told anyone is because my future wife would have to LOVE me for who I really am and not for my money! I know some people might think that if I don't tell my future wife how rich I am then I am lying to her. But I don't look at that as lying, I look at it as.... My future wife needed to LOVE me for what I am in, in my real name, and not my other life. Once, I was married, well then I would have told my wife, "By the way, I am also a millionaire." However, now that my life might be on the line because I don't know what these cops will do to me, well I want the world to know who my brother and I were before the police try to ruin our name again. I am telling everyone my secrets so the police don't say I was doing illegal things so don't believe what I have to say. But now you will know the truth about me and you can come up with your own conclusion.

The other reason I kept my double life a secret is because I don't report my gambling winnings. There are a lot of poker players that do pay their taxes so I do not represent them. I chose not to pay for my taxes because I wanted to live a private life and for some other reasons. However, after this book goes public, I will start paying more of my taxes. Also it is illegal in the state of Washington to play poker on-line now, but there is ways around that.

I know the (reader) is thinking, well (I am a criminal) because I don't pay all my taxes. Well, in my real name, I do pay all my taxes. However, I use different "user" names to play poker and I don't pay all my taxes off my fake names. I pay my taxes when I buy a house, I pay my taxes when I buy house items, but the only taxes I don't pay are the taxes I don't report off my gambling winnings. If I lose 100,000 dollars because of gambling, I can't take that off my taxes. However, if I make $100,000 off gambling and report my winnings then I have to pay a lot of taxes. But I can't get money if I lose money. Why do you think I don't pay all of my taxes? I rather spend my money helping people instead of someone else using my money and who knows what those tax money will be used for. I pay all my taxes when I use my real name, even though I don't make much money off my real name, but I still do the right thing in life.

Since I became really wealthy off playing poker, I knew I could help my brother out, family members, friends, and other people out. I know a lot of people wonder why I didn't put my brother into a mental facility, but that is like putting your parent's in a retirement home at the age of 40 or 50 years old. Also it would be better if our family took care of him because he was a better person when he was around the family.

I got to do a lot of good things with the money I was making off poker. I even met a lot of good people, but I also met some people who weren't so good in life.

One time I was partying at my house in Las Vegas and my ex-girlfriend invited a lot of people. I knew some people at the party were drug dealers, but I told them, "No drugs are allowed in my house." Well one night when we were partying at my house, a guy was overdosing off drugs! I ran on top of him and made him puke up some drugs and then gave him CPR. Then my friend drove us to Emergency room while I was helping the guy out and after two days of being in the hospital, he survived. I found out later in life he was a big drug dealer. We became associates, but not friends. He offered me money or even a job position to make 100K-800K a year, but I refused. I tried to convince him to stop selling drugs and stop using drugs. After I saved his life, he stopped using drugs. Then after two years of stop using drugs, he stopped selling drugs too. Ever since we became good friends and he always told me, "I owe you my life and I would do anything for you." (After he stopped selling drugs, a lot of big time drug dealers were getting killed in Mexico so if he didn't stop selling drugs and if he didn't move then he would have been killed too.) I always thought he was kidding because everyone says "I will do anything for you" to a person in their life time.

I have no problem going to jail for the rest of my life because I am no longer with my brother and I am no longer taking care of my brother. I don't care if I am in jail because I know what will happen next. My associates don't like cops and they have been arrested all their lives too because of their race. They use to do illegal things for a living to make money to take care of their family, but that it is because they were arrested many times for things they didn't do. The reason they became criminals was because they kept on getting arrested for no reason and then they had a criminal history. Then they couldn't get a decent job growing up so they started to sell drugs to make money. They were really good at their job and they use to just set up meetings to sell the drugs and they use to make over a half a million dollars per year. I hardly ever hanged out with these people after I found out what they did for a living, but the reasons why I would hang out with them, was to try to convince them to stop selling drugs. Also one day I found out they had the connections to get some really deadly weapons.

One time when I was hanging out with these associates, they took me to a friend's house. In that house, was a home made basement with some crazy deadly weapons. You could buy pretty much any type of fire arm in that basement. You could buy grenades for $4,000 dollars each and you can even buy a rocket launcher for $240,000 dollars. Also each rocket for the rocket launcher is $50,00 dollars. You could buy bullet proof vest and night vision goggles. So I knew these guys can do some heavy damage, but I told them to not do anything because killing someone is not the answer. However, I really hope I don't go to jail and I really hope these guys don't do something stupid if something happens to me. During the time I was wealthy, I did the following to help people.

My achievements

1. Paid for a friend's vacation because he couldn't afford to take a vacation. (He was making less than 17K a year so I told him that I couldn't go on my vacation because I was working on a new project at work so he should go instead of me.)

2. I took (7) different homeless people to a good restaurant to have a good meal and then I gave them $100 dollars each. (Why would I give them $100 dollars, well because when I look at a person on the streets, I don't judge them and I don't care if they are a drug addicts or a drunks. Not every homeless person is a bad person, they sometimes lose their jobs and everything so they became homeless and they are still human beings and I want to help them.)

3. I took (4) different people to their first MLB baseball

game then paid for dinner, drinks, and got them something at the baseball game so they could remember it. (I usually tell people that my girlfriend family has season tickets and they give me tickets when they can't go to the games.)

4. I take a group of friends or at least one person once a month to a very nice restaurant and pay for their entire meal. (I usually tell people that I have an expense account at work so I will charge my work so that is why I can take them out to dinner.)

5. I helped a friend pay off his tickets from court so he could get his license back. (It sucks when police keep harassing certain type of people so I helped him get his license back.)

6. I have taken (17) different kids to the movies. (I also bought them candy, popcorn, and a soda. There are plenty of families that don't have the extra money to take their kids to see a movie at the theatres.)

7. I paid for two different people to get a lawyer when they had to go to court. (One guy was being charged for robbery and the other guy was being charged for a hit and run. I some times go to court and see people being charged for a crime. I will monitor certain people and by their behavior, their type of clothes, and if I feel a good vibe off them, I will say, "My girlfriend brother is a good lawyer and he doesn't charge anyone any fees because he gets paid by a certain charity to help people out. I give the person a business card of a good lawyer and I pay for his lawyer fees.) When a person has a good lawyer, the defense lawyer can usually negotiate with the prosecutor lawyer to not go to jail, but to pay a big fine. The guy who was being charged

for robbery, well he grabbed his stuff from his ex-girlfriends house, but she called the cops because she didn't want him to have his stuff. The guy who was in a hit and run, well his cousin borrowed the car and hit another vehicle so those are the reason I helped these Human Beings.

8. I let an ex-employee live with me for two months. (His brother stole his money so he couldn't pay for rent and he didn't have a car to go to work so he lived with me until he saved up money to get an apartment with a roommate.)

9. I paid for a bus ticket for a guy to go back home. (One day when I was working at a gas station, a kid was asking people for money around the store. On my break, I asked him where he was from and he told me he was from South Carolina and that he was trying to get money to go back to his parent's house. He moved to Washington State to be with his girlfriend, but they broke up and he didn't have any money or a place to live. He tried to get his parents to give him money, but they were mad at him because he moved far away and they already gave him a lot of money when he moved. And they weren't going to get paid until the end of the week. So after my shift was over, I let him spend the night at my house and then I got him a bus ticket the next morning.)

10. I have picked up over 30 hitchhikers. (Not everyone have money for a car or money to travel) And I am not afraid to pick up a hitch hiker.

11. I have helped (7) people by giving them $50 gift cards for gas. (We all know how much gas cost now and to fill up someone's gas tank is expensive. When I use to work at the gas station, I would tell people that I would always get employee of the month and I got a lot of those $50 dollar

gift cards.)

12. I bought a kid an X-Box 360 with five games. (His family couldn't afford to buy new toys and I told them that I don't use my X-Box 360 anymore.)

13. I have donated blood or plasma over 100 times. (Giving blood or plasma is a really good thing to do because a lot of people need it when they are unhealthy.)

14. I have paid for an entire night of drinks for a group of people. (It gets pretty expensive going out for a night of having a good time. Plus a lot of people need a good night out when they have worked an entire week of hard work.)

15. I paid for (4) different homeless people to live at a hotel for a week. (I did this because most homeless people don't sleep in a shelter and it's nice for them to not live in the streets for a week.)

16. I paid for a woman's groceries one day. (She was in line in front of me and she forgot her little purse that carried her money. She had a big purse, but after looking for 15 minutes and then searching her car, she came back to line and told the clerk that she forgot her money. So I said, "Mam, not to be rude, but I want to pay for your groceries." She thought I was crazy and she refused, but then I took my wallet out and showed her my big stack of $100 dollar bills and said, "I am a lot richer than you may think and I like to help people out even if they don't need it." I could tell this woman didn't have much money and she had her son with her and her son really wanted his candy so I ended up paying for her groceries.)

17. I anonymously donated $25,000 dollars to a friend's medical bills. (He had cancer so I got a lot of people to donate money to pay for his bills.)

18. I helped a person give her son a great birthday party. (I paid for a theme party of "Thomas the train" because the kid's name was Thomas. We got a Thomas the train cake, Thomas the train napkins, Thomas the train plates, and tons of toys of Thomas the train.) The reason I like to help kids have a birthday party is because my family couldn't afford birthday parties or Christmas parties so I know how important it is to give a kid something special for a birthday or a Christmas day.

19. I stopped giving homeless people cash so I gave (4) different homeless people $100 gift cards for Wal-Mart.

20. I paid for a friend to go to Europe after her divorce. (Her ex-husband cheated on her with her best friend and got her best friend pregnant. One of her dreams was to go to Europe for a month so I paid for her ticket to go to Europe. I explained to her since I traveled so much, I could get free tickets for her to go to Europe. So she went and brought me a bottle of liquor from Germany.)

21. I helped two homeless people get an apartment, get a job, and get a car. (I lied to them by saying to them that I won the lottery a long time ago and I have a lot of time and money so I want to help people.)

22. I bought my ex-girlfriend nephew football tickets for his birthday and the tickets were right behind first row. (I also gave him $100 dollars because his family couldn't afford the tickets and couldn't afford to pay for parking and so he could buy something at the football stadium. I told my ex-girlfriend that I was going to visit my family at the time and since I wasn't going to see the game, it would be best his nephew used the tickets because he loved football.)

23. A lot of family members and friends needed money to

pay bills so I would lend them money. (Some people need to borrow money so I would lend them money and I wouldn't care if I got paid back.)

24. I got plane tickets for a friend and her kids to see her family in Colorado in which she hasn't seen a long time. (I told her that I was going to Colorado and that my job was paying for my expenses.)

25. I have given (3) different families a $500 gift card to Wal-Mart for a Christmas present because these families were living in a small camp where they don't make much money. (I also meet a lot of people at food banks and whenever I am in line with them, I evaluate the car they drive, the type of clothes they are wearing and the way they talk to people. Once, I feel a good vibe feeling about a person, I will say, "I know this is going to sound weird, but I give random people gift cards because I like to do nice things for people. I show them the card and the receipt. A lot of people who I try to help out, sometimes think I am making up a lie or there is a hidden camera or I want something from them. However, I never ask for anything, I just want to help people out. I actually had over 20 different people refuse my gifts because they think its a joke or something has to be illegal, but I am just trying to be a good person.)

26. I took (3) different people on helicopter rides in Las Vegas, California, and New York. (Even though these people lived in those cities, they never really experienced how they saw their cities in a helicopter ride so they had a great night. I paid dinner at a nice restaurant and then went drinking at different bars around the city. It only cost between $400 to $600 dollars for a helicopter ride for two human beings. It's a nice time and I always recommend

people to do it because you see the city you live in, in another way and the view is usually phenomenal.)

27. I paid for a family's house payment for two months. (I knew a guy who got laid off from work and he couldn't find work because of the economy. His wife didn't work and she couldn't find work either. He ran out of unemployment money so I told him that I won $10,000 dollars from the lottery and I wanted to help him out. I told him he could slowly pay me back when he found a job. His wife cooked me a great dinner meal, spaghetti and meatballs, yum, yum, and after the two months, he found a new job and slowly paid me back. Even though I didn't want the money, some people don't like to not pay people back so he paid me back in full.)

28. Every time I would move around in Seattle, I would give most of my stuff to "Good Will" and buy new stuff for my new apartment or house.

29. I gave a an ex-employee a nice plasma TV. (One time she came over to my house for a Bar B Q and saw all my big screen televisions and she never had the money to buy a nice television so the next week I told her I won a contest and got a nice big plasma television and since I already had two televisions at my house, I gave it to her. So she bought me coffee for the next two weeks.)

30. I bought a group of people a nice bottle of wine. (One time I was at a wine tasting winery with my ex-girlfriend and before I left, I told our host I would like to buy everyone a bottle of wine and to say, "Congratulations everyone, you are our 10,000 group to come to our winery so please have one bottle of wine of your choice on us, but no more than $200 dollars. Overall, I paid $2300 dollars for that day. My

ex-girlfriend at the time didn't know I did that because when she went to the restroom and I told our host what I wanted to do and I gave her $3000 dollars in cash.)

31. I still donate money to kids in other countries who don't have the opportunity that I have. (I even flew to Africa one time and met a kid that I sponsor.)

32. Every time I went on a vacation, I would bring back some gifts for family and friends.

33. I gave (2) $500 Wal-Mart gift cards to a poor family. (I put them in the mail box where people lived in a old beat up mobile home.)

34. I bought a person an IPod for a birthday gift. (I was invited to a birthday party so I brought a gift to be generous.)

35. I gave an ex-employee $800 dollars because she was getting evicted from her apartment. (Her car broke down and she had to borrow money to fix the car and she was two months behind her rent so I paid it off so she could keep working and live in a good place.)

36. I bought a very nice couple their dinner. (One time when I was eating at a nice restaurant, my waiter told me he was busy with the couple who are celebrating their 45 years of marriage. So I told him to send them a nice bottle of wine and I would pay for their dinner. After the couple found out what I did, they came to my table and thanked me for my generous offer. Then they sat down, we drank more wine, and then they told me how they met. They met in high school and they had three girls and seven grand children. They were still madly in LOVE like the day they got married.) I some times go out and eat alone to observe people.

37. I set up and paid for a divorce bachelor party for a really good friend. (He was going through a rough time in life because his ex-wife divorced him and took his two kids to live six hours away from him.)

38. I took (6) different people to their favorite singer's concerts and the tickets were always in front row or second row. (It was a great experience for these people because they never went to a concert or they never went to a concert of their favorite singer in front row seats. I even took them shopping for that special day, paid for dinner at a nice restaurant, and took a limousine to the concert. I did all that because those people would have one great day in their lives. They couldn't afford that kind of experience, but I did it because I knew they were having a rough time in their lives and they needed a good day.)

39. I took a person to Las Vegas for the weekend because he was dying. (This person was dying of cancer and his doctor told him he only had about three months left to live. So I took him to Las Vegas by getting him a plane ticket, then we got a bad ass room at the MGM Casino, I gave him $10,000 dollars to gamble, I paid for a limousine service for the weekend, we went club hopping and met a lot of girls. I even tried getting another doctor's opinion or other help for him, but unfortunately he died two months later, but at least I gave him one good weekend before he died.)

40. I sponsored a group of kids to have a basketball team for AAU. (I remember when a family gave me $50 dollars so I could join a basketball team.)

41. I helped a person from Mexico get a working Visa to come into the United States. (There are plenty of people in this world that can't find a job in their country so they go to

other countries for work. They are a human being who want to have a better opportunity in life.)

42. I convinced a person to go back to live with his parents. (He ran away and he was living on and off on the streets and he was doing drugs. He thought his parents didn't care about him because they gave him strict rules in the house, but I explained to him that some parent's just show love in different ways so I flew him back home.)

43. I paid to fix a truck. (A gentlemen and his kid entered a auto store to see how much a new transmission would cost for his truck. He didn't know how to speak English that much so I helped him translate and he found out the transmission was too much. So I told him that my dad was a mechanic and he could pay in payments and that my dad gets a really good discounts on parts for vehicles. So I convinced him to drop off the vehicle at my house on a Friday and on Tuesday he picked up the truck. When he wanted to know how much the transmission cost and how much it cost to put the transmission, I told him my dad is a millionaire and he likes to help people out. So he and his wife invited my dad and I to dinner. I went to his house for dinner and I told him that my dad flew to Mexico to see my grandpa. I love Mexican tacos. I had the truck towed to a mechanic and I paid the mechanic to put a new transmission in the truck and we got a three year warranty on the truck.)

44. Once I found out my sister had a heart issue, I gave authorization to my lawyer that if it was necessary then I would give up my heart to my sister and then all my money would be given to my brother in annual payments. (I also had a video message recorded to my brother Alex on what I have done and on why I gave him all my money. I love you

bro and I would have done anything for you.)

45. I upgraded a honeymoon couple to the best hotel suite available. (One time when I went to Paris, a new couple was staying at my hotel and they were so happy checking in the hotel I was staying in. So after they checked in, I checked in right behind them and told the hotel clerk that I wanted to upgrade their hotel room. I told the hotel clerk to tell them, "We made a mistake and all rooms are actually booked except our best room of the hotel! So we would like to give the best room of our hotel on our dime." The hotel clerk came to my room later that night and told me that the couple were jumping up and down when they heard the good news. Then I ended up having dinner with that hotel clerk the next day and we became good friends. I still hang out with her, every time I visit Paris.)

46. I paid 60K for a friend to see her favorite celebrity. (I took her to her singer's concert and while we were there, I told a security guard that I needed to use the restroom because all the men's restrooms were busy. So he let me back stage and my friend and I went to the back stage together. While we were back stage we "accidently" bumped into her favorite singer and they talked for 45 minutes. They took a couple pictures together, she got an autograph microphone, and then we hanged out for an hour after the concert. Through out the years of helping people, I have met people who have the connections of knowing some agents so that is how I set it up.)

47. I gave a homeless person $1000 dollars in cash. (I just won over $130,000 dollars again playing poker one night and I went out to celebrate and I saw a homeless person eating out of the garbage can so I went up to him and said, "Today is your lucky day man." I gave him the money and

he thought it was fake money, but I told him how much money I won playing poker so he hugged me and bought me a couple beers. We started talking for two hours about his life and my life.)

48. I helped pay for a horse's vet bills. (One time I was riding horses with my ex-girlfriend and the owner of the ranch was talking about his horse was extremely sick and he didn't have the money to pay to get the horse better so they would have to let the horse die. So I told my ex-girlfriend to wait in the car and I told the owner of the ranch that I knew a person who helps out people with animals. I told him that someone will come the next day and help him out. So the next day, I went back and gave him $15,000 dollars in cash)

49. I have a bank account set up for my sister just incase something bad happens to me.

50. I have a bank account set up for my dad just incase something bad happens to me.

51. I have a bank account set up for the rest of the family to split up just incase something bad happens to me.

52. I have a bank account set up for six close friends of mine just incase something bad happens to me.

53. I have a bank account set up for a "Mystery person" who helped me change my life just incase something bad happens to me.

54. I bought a college student his books for the semester. (I was at my old college visiting a professor and some student needed money to pay for his books and I told him that my dad was the dean of the college and he pays for one student every year for his books and since he seemed like he really needed the books, I paid it for him. However, I also told

him, "You can't tell anyone because then everyone will ask the Dean to pay or discount the books for college.)

55. I helped out a girl after she found out she was diabetic so I gave her flowers, gift certificate to a spa day for a manicure, a pedicure, a massage, sent her letters of encouragement, and bought her dinner. (However, this girl was different because I really liked her and I wasn't doing it because I was a good guy, I did it because I really wanted to date her, but I screwed up the opportunity because I was really busy and being an idiot during that time.) She was absolutely perfect, she was independent, very outspoken, and had a great job. I gave her a nickname of (R2B) which means... Really 2 Beautiful, this girl was really too beautiful. Every time I saw her beautiful eyes connect with my eyes, it seemed like everything in life was perfect. Every time I saw her beautiful smile while she was talking to me, it seemed like everything in life was perfect. Every time we talked on the phone, it seemed like everything in life was perfect. However, she lived in a different county and like I said before, I messed up the opportunity, but I really do wish her the best in life because she seems perfect and deserves a perfect guy.

56. I helped a person get into rehab for drugs and I paid for his fees. (I hardly have used drugs in my life and I really don't like it when I see a person addicted to a drug because it ruins their life. So one day when I was at an AA meeting, there was a female who gave a good speech that night so I wanted to help her to get off drugs because she lost everything including her two kids that were taken from her. She couldn't take care of her kids so her parent's took her kids because of her drug problem, well after six months of treatment, she got a job, an apartment, stop using drugs, and

got her kids back in a year and a half later!)

57. I sponsored a group of soccer kids to have a AAU team. (A lot of kids every year ask a business to get sponsored so they can play a sport. Wouldn't you want a kid to play some kind of sport instead of trying to experiment in a crime or drugs?)

58. I bought my cousin a very nice 1080i Plasma TV for his birthday gift. (Even though I was going through my horrible time of my life because of my brother's funeral. I wanted to make him happy because his birthday was on my brother's funeral day and he turned 16 and he didn't get much for his birthday. I told my family to not pay me back because I told them I got the television for half price at the job I was working.)

59. The last thing I did that was really good, well I won't say because I sold my house in Las Vegas to help someone out before I started planning on how to harm these fucking coward cops!

Why did I do all this? Well, because my brother taught me a long time ago to not be greedy in life and that we should help each other out. I did a lot of other good things in life, but there are just too many stories to write and maybe one of my other four books is about this? Also, it feels great to help someone who can't afford some things in life. Giving someone a certain thing they can't afford is not a gift, it is my honor I can help out another human being. Do you know how great of a feeling you give someone who works really hard in life, but they can't afford certain things so you help them out so you can change their life for at least one day? I tell a lot of little lies to the people who I am trying to help out because a lot of people don't like to be given things. However, I realized if you tell a little lie to them by saying, "Well I won these tickets, or I won the lottery so I want to share my gifts then more people will accept the gift." Not everyone have the opportunities to be rich in life and we should try to give other people at least one good day in life. In total, I have given over $200,000 dollars to people that I don't know or people I consider friends. I have most of everyone's names that I helped. I have a lot of their phone numbers, email addresses, or their home address.

I have one tattoo in my life and it is the picture of Earth. I put the picture of Earth on my arm because I like to travel the world and see other people's views in life. Also if there is a way I can help a person out in another part of this world, then I will do it because we are all human beings. All my money I make off this book and the rest of my money I have, I am giving it all up to my brother's daughter, my family, and friends. I don't want any money anymore because I don't know what I am going to do. I am 90% suicidal and I don't know how much longer I can last. So I gave up everything I have just incase something happens and the money will help a lot of people's lives.

Number 49 through number 53, I did after my brother's funeral because I really thought I was going to kill myself. The other reason I never told anyone about my money is because I wanted my funeral to be a celebration of life and not a tragedy day. I always figured I would die, but I would invite a lot of people I helped out through out the years and everyone would meet each other and talk about all the things I did for everyone. Then everyone would see a video message from me, on all the things I did and how I did everything to not become rich and famous. I did all the good things so people would understand that I was a Human Being and I wanted to help out other Human Beings.

I always thought my brother Alex would eventually die, but I never analyzed that my brother Alex would get murdered in front of me and then I would be called a liar and a criminal on what I saw that day! That is why till this day, I still think I am in Hell? That is why these cops have no clue on who I am and what I can do.

If I ever went to court for hurting these cops then I will know a lot of these Human Beings will come to my court date and say, "George is a great person, he helped me out even if I didn't ask for it. He would never have hurt these people if they didn't murder his brother and his brother never got justice." So will a jury convict a person who did so many good things in life and I only hurt these "Police Officers" or "Human beings" because they never had to serve time for murdering my brother? If I did have to go to jail for hurting these Police Officers well, I have a back up plan for that and trust me...... It's not a good one.

A lot of people will probably think that since this is a fictional book than I am making all of this up. Well, the number one reason why I am writing this book is because when they police called us liars and saying my brother had a hammer instead of a flashlight, well the truth needs to be told. They insulted my brother and since my brother and I are were one person then I am trying to prove how good of a person my brother was and how good of a person I am in. Since people will always take the cop's side then we need a new system so we can have proof that these cops are doing their job and not abusing their power. So since I don't know how these cops will try to ruin our name again, I have decided to come out of my private life and show..... This time you messed with the wrong human being and you will be caught and all the people who try to cover up this murder will be caught! So this is why I wrote this book!

1. Prove my brother and I were good people

2. Prove that these cops are corrupted

3. Get a new system so cops are being monitored (I know most cop cars have cameras inside their vehicle so why can't we have a camera on a police officer?)

4. Stop cops from harassing, abusing their power, and murdering innocent Human Beings!

5. Remember, they work for us and we don't work for them.

6. Just incase the cops come to arrest me, at least I can show the world that my brother was a good person and I was a good person and they will know my side of the story before the cops ruin my name again!

Like I said before, there are a lot of good cops in the United States, but there are also a lot of bad cops who need to be monitored or fired.

I never understood why so many millionaires always buy a huge mansions or buy multiple homes? Do people really need big houses, luxury cars, and luxury items? I know everyone want the best things in life, but come on.... When I see a person who needs help, even if they don't want help and if I can help them.... Then tell me one good reason why I shouldn't share my wealth? A lot of people are greedy and that is one of the main reasons why this country is in debt.

If you have 50 million dollars, do you really need all that money? I know a lot of rich people give a certain amount of their money to charities, but do you know the money they donate to charities, they just take it off their taxes? So do they really donate money when they can just write it off on their taxes? That is why I rather help people one-on-one because I know I am making a difference. I know a lot of people are saying, "I can do whatever I want with my money." Well, you are 100% right, but there are still human beings in this world who are born in countries where they have no chance to make a living, where they have no chance for education, where they have no choice, but to steal or do illegal things to survive. So if we tried a little bit harder to help each other out than all of us can live in a better world where all of us..... Can be good human beings!

I know a lot of people are wondering why I sometimes live on and off with my dad in his mobile home. Well, I like going back where I grew up because it helps me realize on why I help people for a living. It reminds me how poor I was growing up and I would have loved it, if there was more people like me that would help me out when I was poor. Also if you are wondering how I took care of my brother during this time, well my brother would live on and off with me because he liked living in Eastern Washington to be right next to my mom's grave. He would live in Eastern Washington a lot of the time because he liked talking to my mom at her grave site. So when I wasn't taking care of my brother, I would go out and help other people out because my brother taught me to be a good person.

I wanted to kill these cops....

I was having a really bad time living with my dad after my brother was murdered. I couldn't stay in that mobile home because I couldn't stop having flashbacks of what I saw. So I moved to Eastern Washington for a while, but then I did move back to my dad's mobile home and I started to get a little crazy. So one day, it got really bad and my dad had to handcuff me to my bed. Do you know why my dad had to handcuff me to my bed for two weeks, actually it was for 13 days. It was because I wanted to kill these cops and all the cops who are trying to cover up my brother's murder. I told my dad, I am going to get justice for my brother and I. These fucking cops needed to fucking die and everyone needs to feel my brother's pain and my pain! My dad told me to calm down and to think about it for a while. Then he left and came back with his pastor.

When his pastor came, I was a little shocked. His pastor asked me, "George what do you plan to do?" And I said, "I am going to fucking kill these cops and all the fucking people who are trying to cover this up!" So that is when my dad grabbed me and threw me onto my bed and the pastor jumped on my chest and they both handcuffed me to the bed! I kept on yelling, "Let me go, please let me go and let me go fucking kill these cops! Please, stop doing this and let me go so I can fucking kill these cops!" My dad's pastor kept on preaching from the bible and my dad kept on praying for me, but I kept on yelling, "Stop doing this, please stop doing this, these fucking cops need to feel my pain, they need to feel my brother's pain! Please stop and let me go!" However, my dad and his pastor kept on preaching for me everyday and they would come into the room to feed me and give me water. They kept on preaching to me and telling me that my pain would eventually go away. (My dad will probably deny all this and he should deny it.)

After the 13 days, I was dreaming on how I would kill these cops..... I finally convince my dad and his pastor that I was healed. I told them I was going to go to Eastern Washington to live with my uncle and to be right next to Alex's grave. However, I was dreaming...... I started to drive to California. I grabbed my other phone and drove to an old friend's house. When I got to my friend's house, I told them Plan A was a go and that is when we started planning what I needed to do. The reason I got my other phone is so when the cops start tracing my phone or wonder where I am at, then they can detect from the cell phone towers that I drove to California. However, once I was in California, I started to plan out again on what I was going to do to these cops and everyone who is trying to cover up his murder!

I planned out that I would need a private plane to fly me back home. It cost me $12,000 dollars to go from California to Seattle. I would wear a hat and a wig. I would wear 13 size shoes and shoe lifts in the shoes so it would seem I am taller in the cameras at the airport. I would also wear extra shirts on me so you would think I am very heavy and you couldn't recognize it was me at the airport cameras. Once, I got on the plane I would have a white van waiting for me in Seattle. With the white van, I would put the "Fed Ex" stickers on it so people would think I work for "Fed Ex." Also I already have a "Fed Ex" uniform in my luggage. My "associate" from Las Vegas who use to sell drugs got the social security, home addresses, and pictures of the cops who murdered my brother. My "associate" I already knew what happened to my brother and to me because I told them right away. He has a lot of connections so he started to find out who these cops are and he sent some people to monitor their sleeping patterns, their social life patterns, and their daily life patterns. Trust me when I say this, these kind people who investigate people's daily lives, well they can find out. (How many times a person wipes his or her's ass.)

Once I was back home, I went to a associate's house to pick up some materials in my "disguise". Then I went up to a mountain and then went to a location where nobody goes to. I started digging up the hole on where I would bury the bodies of these fucking coward cops! I drove a long time up the mountain and I found a place where most people don't drive to and where no houses are near at. So then I start digging a hole seven feet deep and four feet wide. It took me a long time to dig these holes because it's pretty hard to dig up a big hole by yourself. In the "Fed Ex" van, I had body bags and I put "Fed Ex" stickers on the body bags just incase someone saw me leaving a house with a bag over my shoulder. Also I took everything out of the van and put a plastic cover in the back of the van. And I would always wear latex gloves and my disguise when I was doing everything.

The way I was going to kill these cops.... Well, the day of when I was going to do it, I had two latex gloves on, my wig on, a fake beard on, color eye contacts, my big shoes on with extra weight inside them, I put on some white make up on so you would think I was Caucasian, I put shoe lifts so I could seem taller, I shaved my entire body so no hair would be left at the crime scene, I had a gun with a silencer, I cleaned all the bullets and I always wore gloves when putting bullets in the gun, I had a box to carry to the house (the box was something that the cop would think he was getting a delivery from Fed Ex), inside the box was a fire extinguisher, the body bag, handcuffs, rope, and more ammo for my gun. If someone else was in the house, I wouldn't kill them, I would just tie them up so they couldn't get away.

After I would have killed the first cop, I would have gone straight to the location where the other cop was at and I would have done the same thing. The reason I brought a fire extinguisher to the crime scene is for many reasons. First, after I shot and killed the cops. There would be blood and possibly DNA from me on the crime scene. I would pick up any shell casings at the crime scene then I would use the fire extinguisher where the body was lying on the ground and if I was sweating then the fire extinguisher would ruin the crime scene. Also if I walked over the area of the fire extinguisher then the police detective can measure the criminal's shoe length, they wouldn't be my size. I would put the bodies into the hole and put a certain material over the body so the smell and bodies couldn't be detected.

After I killed those two cops, I would have gotten rid of the white van by cleaning it up and crushing it a at junk yard. Then I would have met another associate. He would have stolen two cars that day and he would have a line of spikes, two assault rifles, six grenades, a tape recorder, five gallons of gas, a fire extinguisher, bullet proof vest, night vision goggles, body armor, a black helmet, and a my other disguise in the first vehicle. He would have gone to the other side of the city with a tape recorder with a women's voice on it and with his disguise he would have gone to a public phone. On the public phone he would have called 911 with the woman's voice saying, "Please come to the location, (shots fired in the background) someone is shooting a guy!) Then one of the police stations that killed my brother would go across town at 7PM. So most of the police officers would head across town to find out who is shooting a gun! Then with one of the stolen cars, my other disguise and my body suit, I would have placed the line of spikes on the street so no car can chase me down. I then would have used the fire extinguisher to place on the spikes so no DNA is on them and to cover the spikes. I then would have started throwing grenades at the police station and started firing over 300 shots with the assault rifle at the police station.

After all the devastation I would have gone to the next car location. I would have burned down the car with the ten gallons of gas and the other two grenades. I would have driven the next car to the private plane area. The second car had two other assault rifles with a lot of ammo, a lot of grenades, and the ROCKET LAUNCHER so we could make it to the private plane. My other associate would have burned down the other stolen car. Then at the barn we were at, we had a tunnel to a certain location. From that location we would have ran to the private plane and gone back to California. Once we were back in California, our associates would have started video recording us going out to the clubs to party. We would act like nothing exciting was going on and everything seemed "Normal?"

During this time, I already recorded my voice and it said the following, "Hey, what's up it's George and I am in California for a while, but I will be back soon, oh wait, let me call you back in a minute." My other associates would have called someone with that message to a family member in Lynden while I was doing these crimes. Also they would have texted some friends and some family members during this time so people would think I was in California and if the police would have checked my phone log then they would see I was in California. I also bought a big bottle of clear vodka and my associated video recorded me drinking a lot of vodka that morning, but we emptied the bottle of vodka and put water in it. Then I would pass out on my bed and people would think I was too drunk to do anything that day. So I flew back to Seattle in the private plane and then I would have flown back to California that same day in the private plane. My associates would have said I was there the entire time and I would have phone records, a video recorded message, and I would have two people who claim I was with them. So I could have gotten away with murder and one of the biggest crimes in History!

However, the morning I was suppose to do all that, well I entered the white van and something really weird and I mean something really weird happened.........

When I got inside that white van that morning, all of sudden I felt this big weight on my shoulders and I couldn't move. Then my brother Alex appeared on the passenger seat. So I was in complete shock and I thought it wasn't real? So I said, "Alex,..... Is that really you?" and he said, "What are you doing?!" So I said, "Well...." He then said, "Be quiet and just listen because I don't have much time, you are better than this and even though you can get away with these murders, God, me and our mom will know you did this. A lot of people will think some Mexican did all those murders and everything I taught you would have been a wasted! I know I am not here anymore to be with you, I know you are in a lot of pain, but believe me and trust me when I say this, all this pain will go away! You have a great gift and you are a really good person so please don't do this! The Devil is controlling your mind right now because you are not this person! Remember your number one goal in life.....? It's to go to Heaven and to meet our mom. She has been watching us from time to time and she is really proud on what you have done, she really LOVES you, but God showed us what you were going to do and that is why I am here, but if you do this, YOU WILL NOT BE ABLE TO SEE HER." Then he put his left arm on my right shoulder and all of sudden we were in another place.

I didn't recognize this place because it was a dark place and there was a lot of lightning in the sky. The sky was red, orange, and some black with no clouds. The ground was a weird brown color and I saw a gate in front of me. When I tried to talk to Alex he said, "Don't talk, let me show you this because we don't have much time." So we started walking towards the gate and the ground was shaking like it was an earthquake. Some of the ground would crack and the lightning would get worst when we got closer to the gate. When we got closer to the gate, I kept on hearing weird screaming from people like people were being tortured? The gate was a pure bright red color and there was blood dripping on some parts of the gate. Then we got about five feet away from the gate, and Alex said, "This is the gate of Hell." So I got scared and I started to run away, but that is when my brother grabbed me and said, "This isn't for you, this gate is for the people who killed me and all the people who do evil things. But if you kill these cops, you will go there too and you won't be able to see our mom and you won't be able to see me ever again!" So then my brother put his face in front of my face and said, "You are a good person so show people on who you really are, show people we are human beings! I love you bro so don't kill these cops." Then my brother put his left arm on my right shoulder again and then I was back in the white van.

I thought I was either dreaming or something really weird just happened. I wasn't drinking or doing any type of drug that day so I still don't know what happened that day was real? My brother was wearing a plain white t-shirt and plain white pants. So then I started crying and then I knew what I had to do. I went back to the hole that I dug up and covered it up. I went to a different area and burned all the items I had. I then took off the "Fed Ex" sticker from the van and cleaned up the van. I took the van far away and I had it crushed in a junk yard. I told my associates what I was doing so we went back to California and told my other associates that I didn't do it. I also told them what happened and they understood and said, "Well, trust me, we won't tell anyone about this and we are taking off to another country just incase something happens and then the police can't get us. Well email us if you want to go there and we can set everything up and you can retire there with us."

I then went back home and I didn't tell anyone until right now. I know the cops will try to investigate this because they can put me in jail for plotting to kill these cops, but the truth during those 13 days of being handcuffed, I was thinking so many evil things and I was planning how I could kill these cops, but when I convinced my dad to let me go and when I got into my car.... That is when I saw a vision of my brother in my white BMW. However, the cops will try to investigate and put me in jail so I have to write the following.

1. First this book is fictional so everything I say in this book isn't real.

2. You have to find the materials that I had to do this,

but you won't because they are gone.

3. You have to find my associates, but you won't find them.

4. Did I want to kill these cops, Yes, but prove to the court system that I was going to do it. Also since this is a fictional book, I can say whatever I want to say, "Of course these cops should die and I was fantasizing, and writing a good fictional book?"

5. I will deny everything and I will say I made up everything because I am crazy.

6. I can't believe my brother didn't want me to hurt these people, but he is 100% right and I will not kill these cops. (So the cops who murdered my brother and the people who covered up his murder.... You are so lucky my brother and I are good people.)

7. If I do go to jail for the rest of my life, well at least you know the truth about my brother and I.

8. If I do go to jail, I will try to help people who are in jail to try to have a better life once out of prison. I will try to help them realize they don't need to do a crime and there are better ways to live a good life.

I know a lot of family members and friends will not want to talk to me anymore, but I can live with that. I can live with the fact if the police come after me and try to put me in jail. At least I am trying my best to make sure justice is served and more. When the police come to arrest me and try to interrogate me, well then I will give them my list of people that I have helped out through out the years. They will investigate and find these people and realize how much of a good person I was.

1. Their names

2. Email addresses

3. Dates and times when I helped them out

4. Phone numbers

5. Home address

6. I will give them my different names that I have used and show them how I was living a double life.

7. However, if they come and kill me, I will have a lot of video recorders in my car and every where I go so people can realize I didn't have a gun or weapon when the police were trying to arrest me or kill me.

When I am at the police station being interrogated, I will give them my account number where I have a lot of money in, then I will have one of my associates transfer that money into another account. The reason I will transfer the money into another account is so the police or government don't try to freeze my account or make me pay for the taxes that I didn't pay. Then I will give them the Police Officer #1 and Police Officer #2 first five digits of their social security number. So once they know how much money I have and then they will know I have the connections to get the police officers social security numbers. Once you have a person's social security number then you can find practically anything about that person. What do you think the police will think then? Probably, "Holy shit, this guy is good person, but now he is pissed off and he can hurt someone if he really wants to. So do we go after him and try to put him in jail and piss him off even more?"

I don't need the cop's money or what I call it, "Their sorry money or their blood money." I am going to give any money I get to my brother's daughter. I have been arrested over 15 times and when I mean arrested, I mean handcuffed and questioned about a crime. I could have sued the police and the city for harassment and for falsely arresting a person, but I don't need the cop's money to survive. I have written four other books in my life, but I am not going to mention my books names because I don't need to make money promoting those books. I also have written a TV script, a movie script, and done so many other things! I can make a living without suing the city or the police for harassment!

1. I was arrested / handcuffed for running home after football practice and the cop thought I robbed a house.

2. I was arrested / handcuffed because I dropped off my brother at his friend's house and the cops pulled me over after I dropped off my brother. The cop wanted to know where my drugs were at because they have been monitoring my brother's best friend's house for over three months and the cop said, "We know that kind of people sells drugs because there a lot of Mexicans that go in and out of that house." My brother's friend didn't sell drugs, a lot of his friends who happen to be Mexican, went over to their house because they had a big screen T.V. and they would play Nintendo 64. So I let the officer search my car and he found nothing, but I was still arrested because I was 15 years old and I didn't have a license at that time.

3. My dad and I were arrested / handcuffed because when I had to go to court for not having a license, well we were pulled over by the same cop who gave me the ticket for not having a license. When the cop told us why he pulled us over, he told my dad and I, "You didn't have your seat belt on and one of your brake light isn't working." My

dad didn't understand English that much so when I explained to him why we were pulled over, we showed him that we had our seat belts on and we stepped outside the car and checked the brake lights. The brake lights were working fine, but the cop still gave us a ticket. I started to yell at the cop and he handcuffed me until another cop came on scene. We explained to the other cop what happened so he convinced the cop to let us go and then we went to court. When we arrived to court late, we showed the judge the new ticket and showed him our brake lights. The judge told us he would investigate the cop so two weeks later, the judge sent a letter that we didn't have to pay for the ticket.

4. I was arrested / handcuffed because one day I took off from my house to drive down the street to the store. I only brought cash on me and when the police officer pulled me over for going 27 MPH on a 25 MPH zone, he arrested me because I was 17 and I didn't have my license on me. I told the cop, we can go down the block to get my license, but he said, "No, I won't do that because if your people saw me bring you to your house, then your people will try to jump me." I just started to laugh and said, "You are an idiot." So my dad had to bring my license to the police station and pick me up.

5. I was arrested / handcuffed because a cop pulled the "Police tactic" when I was pulled over because my windows seemed to have illegal tinted windows. The officer said, "I smell marijuana." So I let him search my car and after 30 minutes of searching my car, I got really bored and put my hands in my pockets. Then the police officer got scared and pulled his gun on me. He then said, "Put your hands out of your pocket slowly." I didn't have baggy or big pants, they were normal tight pants so I had nothing in my pants. I just

got bored and put my hands in my pockets. So after I got my hands out of my pocket, the officer put me in handcuffs and kept searching my car. After another 20 minutes of searching my car, he finally uncuffed me and let me go.

6. I was arrested / handcuffed because my friend and I left a night club. My friend got a girl's phone number, but her ex-boyfriend got mad because he was white so three of his friends tried to jump my friend and I. We ended up beating up the four white guys and when the police came on scene, the police right away arrested my friend and I. We were put in the cop car without questions because when the police arrived, two of the guys were still on the ground passed out and the other two guys ran up to the police and told them that we had knives. So the cops arrested us and searched for weapons. It wasn't until the security guard told the cops what really happened and showed them on their security camera on what happened, then the cops let us go.

7. I was arrested / handcuffed one night when I was drinking with my friends on the roof of his apartment. When my friends ran out of beer, they went down stairs back to their apartment to grab more beer. I decided to go back to the apartment to see why my friends are taking so long and when I was walking down stairs, two cops grabbed me and arrested me. They told me I was being arrested for burglary? I was trying to explain to them that I was on the roof with my friends drinking and I was just going back to their apartment to see what's going on. Then my friend came out of his apartment and told the police I was with him all night so they let me go.

8. I was arrested / handcuffed because some malls don't allow a group of "Mexicans" or groups of "Minorities" to walk around some malls in the United States. So when

the security officer told us that we need to walk in a set of two or a set of three and not walk in a group then we told them, "Fuck you, we aren't fucking gang members and you wouldn't do this if we were white!" So they called the cops and the cops handcuffed us and told us the rules of the mall and then let us go.

9. I was arrested / handcuffed for being drunk in public, but they released me.

10. I was arrested / handcuffed because the day my hand was cut on a mirror, I went to the hospital for stitches and to put a splint on my hand. The doctor gave me a prescription for vicodin so when I went to the pharmacy wearing a big puffy jacket because it was cold and raining that night. Well after giving the pharmacist the prescription, my name was called 45 minutes later and when I went to the counter to pick up my prescription, two police officers grabbed me and arrested me! Since my right hand was still bleeding and had a splint, the officer had to put the handcuff on my left hand to the back of my pants. The officer kept on saying, "Who do you work for? Who gave you this fake prescription?" And I kept on yelling back at the officer, "I just left the fucking hospital man, look at my bleeding arm and go inside my car and you can see all my medical papers." But he didn't care and he put me in the cop car and I was taken to the police station. They took a picture of me and finger printed me. He didn't give me a ticket that night because he said they would have to investigate if I was telling the truth. Then after I was let go that night at (1 A.M) I had to walk nine miles back to the pharmacy to my car in the pouring rain. The next day I went back to the police station and showed him all my medical bills and a copy of the prescription that my doctor gave me.

I could have sued the pharmacy for not calling the hospital to check if the prescription was real and I could have sued the cops by not investigating the truth, but I didn't sue them because I don't need their money to survive.

11. I was arrested / handcuffed because I use to live right next to the Green Lake park in Seattle and sometimes I would jog at 11pm at night. Well one night after I got done running six miles, I was running home and a cop pulled in front of me. The cop looked at me once and then put the handcuffs on me. He said, "You are being arrested for robbing the house down the road." And I was in complete shock because I had a sweater and sweat pants, but I also had a boxing training sweat uniform underneath my clothes to help me work out more. So when the cop wanted to see my license, I said, "Look man, I just got done running six miles and if you take off my sweater, you will see my boxing suit. I don't have my license because I was jogging so I don't carry my wallet." So after 30 minutes talking to the officer and when another officer came on scene, he realized I was a jogger and not a robber so they finally let me go.

12. I was arrested / handcuffed for a D.U.I and I am 100% guilty for that!

13. I was arrested / handcuffed because I use to live right next to the store where I managed and I saw a bunch of cop cars surround the store where I worked. So I walked to the store (3 A.M.) and asked what the cops were doing and they right away arrested me and asked me if I robbed the store? I told them that I work at the store and I live just down the street, but they didn't believe I was the manager or that I lived down the street. So we tried calling my boss or my assist manager, but since it was (3 A.M.) nobody

picked up the phone. The cops took me down to the police station and they put me in a small white room and interrogated me for over three hours. They kept on saying, "Just admit the truth and we won't charge you. We know you robbed the store so just tell us the truth." I kept on telling them to go to my house to pick up the keys of the store and I wouldn't break the windows to rob the store. Plus I put the money we make in the bank after we close the store, so there isn't money in the store! However, the cops still didn't believe me until my boss called the police back at (7 A.M) so the cops released me and I had to walk five miles back to my house. And to make the night even worst, my car that I park at the store so I don't have to pay for parking, well it was stolen that night! I could have sued the cops, but I didn't because I don't need their money to survive.

14. I was arrested / handcuffed because my friends and I use to play poker every night at my apartment. Somebody complained that we must have been drug dealers because a lot of people go in and out of my apartment at night. So when the officers monitored my apartment, well one day the officer came to my door and said, "We know you are doing illegal things in here and I can get a search warrant and make you stay out of your apartment until I have the search warrant. The best thing to do is for you to hand me the drugs and you won't get much in trouble." So first I said, "Well first of all sir, I know the laws and you can't make me do anything. If you have a search warrant then you can enter my apartment, but since I don't do illegal drugs then you can enter my house right now and search my place! So one police officer handcuffed me and then searched my apartment. They kept on telling me, "Just tell

us where the drugs are at so we can help you out." But I just kept on laughing because my friends would come over because I had two big screen televisions in my apartment and I had two X-Box 360s and we would play on-line all night long or play poker all night. After the cops found nothing, they released me and never came back.

15. I was tackled off my brother while giving him CPR. Then my brother was rolled over and handcuffed after he was shot at 13 times! And then my dad and I were put on the ground to search for guns or weapons! Are you freaking serious? Is this how cops are trained to do their job? If this happened to you, what kind of justice would you want?

Of all the times, I have been arrested / handcuffed, I have only been proven Guilty one time! I have all the dates and times when I have been arrested or handcuffed. I have been arrested in Washington, California, Texas, Colorado, New York, and Florida. I always thought I had bad luck in life with cops, but I have met so many other minorities that have gone through the same kind of things. I even met an African American guy who kept on getting pulled over by his neighbor cop. He got tired of being pulled over so he started riding the bus to work. Even his friends would get pulled over for no reason when they went to his house. Every time they made a complaint to the police, they would say, "If the officer gives you a ticket, you can fight it at court." It wasn't until one of his friends put a hidden camera in his car and when he got pulled over for speeding, he showed the judge at court that he wasn't speeding and then the cop was investigated. A couple months later the guy found out, that the officer got suspended and not fired!

If you ask one out of four minorities if they ever been arrested or handcuffed for no reason, I guarantee they will say YES! Either cops really suck at their jobs or they use stupid tactics to arrest innocent minorities! Why do you think there are more Mexicans and African Americans in Jail than any other race? It is because we get profiled and we get harassed all the time! I know a lot of my friends just say, "Well fuck it, if cops are always harassing me of being a criminal then I should become a criminal." I know that sounds stupid, but when you get a conviction on your criminal history for no reason, what are you suppose to do then?

What will happen when we are no longer the minority and the Caucasian become the minority? I don't want to sound racist because I am not a racist, but if you don't want this to happen to your future kids or your future grand kids then we need to have cops to have video cameras on their uniforms so we can make them stop abusing their power. I know the police department or the government will say, "The police have a hard job, it will cost too much, or they are just using police tactics." I respect good cops, but I don't respect corrupted cops who abuse their power and try to arrest innocent people.

Letters to family and friends

Sister

I know you probably won't ever talk to me again, but I had to write this book so the truth comes out. I don't care what happens to me, but I am tired of cops abusing their power and every year nobody can change anything. I know you won't understand what I am doing, but that is because Alex and I did everything together growing up. He was the person who made me become a great person and I was the one who was suppose to take care of him. And these cops killed Alex and they killed me! No matter what happens from now on, I will no longer be George.

I am sorry that I never told you what I have accomplished in my life. I know you always paid for my lunch or dinner when we went out, but that was because it feels great to be appreciated by another family member. I am really happy that you would help me out even though you didn't need to help me out. Even though you lived in Eastern Washington and didn't grow up with my brother Alex and I, it was weird that I didn't know I had you as a sister until later on in life. I do have issues with trusting people, but that is because you didn't see the things that my brother and I had to deal with. Every time you paid for a lunch or any time you let me borrow a couple of bucks, I set up an account and put all the money that you helped me through out the years in that account. I also doubled it and I was going to give it to you when you retired so you can see how much of a good person I was. However, since after Alex was murdered and since Alex told me what to do. I wrote this book to tell the truth. I don't know if you will ever talk to me again and I will respect your decision. I don't know what the police will try to do against me, but I wanted to tell you the truth just incase the police try to kill me or put me in jail for writing this book. Also if they do put me in jail, don't bail me out. Let me live my life in jail and enjoy your life by helping out other people.

This is why I never showed you the other books that I have written. Like I said before I am an anonymous writer because if you have read those books than you would know the things that I know, how smart I am, you would know how many books I sold, and how much money I have. I just wanted to feel normal around you and it's a great feeling when you would help me out when you didn't need to. It shows you have a great soul and you are like my brother and I, we want to help people out.

Brother

To my oldest brother: You moved away from Alex and I when we were kids to live in Eastern Washington. You were always in and out of jail, but you did change my life in a positive way. I saw all of your mistakes and I learned from them. I didn't get addicted to drugs because of you and Alex. I saw how much it ruined your lives so I didn't get addicted to drugs and I became a good person. I have tried so many times to stop people using drugs because I know how painful it is to see family members using drugs. If you are wondering why I am doing this, well you remember that day we got shot at by that Nazi and we didn't get any help from the police. It's been almost 20 years from that day and cops are still being corrupted. I have been harassed all my life and I have met so many other people in this country that get harassed and arrested for no reason. You know what they did to Alex and it is time for someone to step up and show the world that we need to change. Also I wanted to show the world that Alex and I were "Good guys."

Dad

We had a very weird life growing up. However, you never saw what Alex and I were doing when were hanging out. We became one person relying on each other to live a good life. I know you tried your hardest to take us to church every week and you tried to make us pray every night, but once we were old enough we stopped going to church. We stopped praying every night and we hardly spoke to you growing up. However, you didn't fail us with our family, you did what you could to survive in this world. We know you worked really hard growing up in the rain, in the snow, in the wind, and some times in the hot weather. We know you made mistakes from time to time just like everyone else, but I became a good person because you taught Alex to teach me to be a good person. I didn't tell you on how much money I had because I like being normal around the family. Also, when it was going to be your 60th birthday, I was going to surprise you with a lot of money so you could retire.

I know you are a very religious person and I still don't understand how you can be so strong with a religion. I don't understand how you can be so strong after you were in between the two officers that killed Alex. But I guess you believe in God so much that he helps you heal in life. I still remember one of the most funny days in my life. We were on the freeway coming back from California and two skin head guys pulled up next to our van and both of them were flipping us off. Then one of the guys pointed a gun at us and you grabbed your bible in the van and you pointed it out the window. The two guys were stunned and just drove away. I laughed so hard because I was thinking, "Those guys had a gun and my dad only had a bible?" But it is true, some people are more afraid of a Bible than a gun. However, you need to understand that some people don't believe in God and will lie. I have been telling you every day since Alex was murdered that these cops will not tell the truth. I know you keep on saying, "They will tell the truth, just wait they will tell the truth." Dad, they are not going to tell the truth because not everyone is religious so you need to understand that these cops will not go to jail. I have accepted they won't go to jail, but I know they will go to Hell. However, you got me really mad when you tell me that these cops can repent and still go to Heaven. Well, that is one thing I won't understand. I love you dad, but we all have our different beliefs.

Close friends

I will understand if you won't want to talk to me or hang out with me anymore. Most of my friends know how I grew up. The reason I didn't tell anyone how rich or smart I am is because...... I like being around my friends and feel "Normal." I like feeling being one of the guys. I know sometimes I would do stupid things from time to time, but that was because you would think I am a clown and not someone who has lots of money. I know a lot of you guys or girls will say, "You could have trusted me and you could have told me everything you do." But like I said before, I like hanging out with my friends without people knowing how much money I have. I never had a normal childhood because a lot of people knew how smart or athletic I was. I want a "Normal" life so I didn't tell anyone what I have been doing.

Remember, I changed my phone number every six months? Remember, sometimes I would ask you to call me by a different name? Remember, that I would always be driving a different car every six months to a year? Remember how many crazy stories I have told you on the gambling winnings I have done. But you never thought I have been playing on-line and winning a lot of money. I never wanted anyone to know what I am doing because I am not looking for people to thank me for the things I do. I just wanted to be a "normal" guy around my friends and I didn't want to be treated different if you knew all the things I have done. I know a lot my friends are going to say, "What the fuck man? Is that why you always traveled and you were going to different places? Is that why you were always doing something weird?"

To my minority friends, we all have some time in our

lives been arrested or harassed by cops and I am writing this book for my brother and for myself, but most importantly, I am writing this book for all the people have been arrested or harassed and we couldn't do anything to stop it. We as a nation need to stand up and say enough is enough.

I will respect your decision if you don't want to talk to me anymore. I don't know what the cops will do next, but I know they will probably be monitoring me for the rest of my life. I know they will probably interrogate a lot of my friends and they will probably threaten some of my friends to get bad information about me. They will probably say, "If you don't help us, then we can arrest you for some bull shit law." However, they can't arrest you, but it's there way to try to make someone who doesn't know the laws to find out information for them. So all I ask, tell them anything you know about me and you then you will be left alone.

People who I helped

I don't know if the police will come and investigate you to find out what I have done, but if they do, they will show you a picture of me and my real name. I will give them all the different names that I have used and all I ask is for you to tell the truth on what I did to help you. They will probably want some bad information about me to make me look like a bad person, but just tell them anything you know about me. You are not in trouble because you didn't know where the money was coming from and I was the person who bought the gifts or other stuff. The police can not arrest you for the stuff I gave you.

Devil

You are a very smart, but evil thing. You were very close on bringing me to your side. I still have to handcuff myself to my bed on some nights because I am afraid of what I will do. I know maybe after years and years of counseling that maybe I will get part of my mind to be somewhat "Normal" again, but I also know you will try to play games with me. I know I have done a lot of evil things too, but I am a good person because I have done a lot of things to help people out. I am not sure where I will end up, but if I do end up in Hell then I will fight as hard as I can so you can feel my pain. There will be a good person in Hell if I end up in your world, but I will also bring my brother's and my pain down there.

God

I still don't understand why my brother was so brutally murdered, but I guess everything happens for a reason? I was very serious on what I did on my brother's funeral and I am pretty sure that is why you sent my brother to talk to me. I am completely lost on what I am suppose to do with my life because I always thought Alex would be around. I some times still think I am in Hell because nothing make sense? After all the good things I have done, I just don't understand why this happened? I know I don't pray every night and I hardly ever go to church, but I still try my best to help people. I know I won't be the kind of person who goes to church every Sunday because I believe if I do good things and pray once in a while then I should be OK. However, I will do my best to go to church more often.

Please God, help me stop thinking evil things. I need your help more than ever because I am tired of being harassed, I am tired of being arrested, while my brother was murdered, I was almost murdered too so there has to be a reason why I didn't get murdered that day and I believe it is because I am writing this book and to have these cops put video cameras on their uniform. I believe now, once people read this book and start reading how much police are abusing their power, then they need to put video cameras on them because we are the United States of America and we are suppose to be the Land of the Free and be the land of helping others so why can't we show the world, "We are all human beings!"

Thank you Lord for everything you have given me and I really hope I can be that good person I once was so I can have the opportunity to go to Heaven to see my brother again and to eventually see my Mom.

Mom

I am so scared in my life right now. I thought all the good things I was doing would stop evilness to enter our world. I never hit a cop or did anything to piss them off. Every time they have tried to ruin my life, I would always walk away and not fight back. However, after what they did to Alex and what they did to me.... It's really hard for me to not do anything! I am tired of cops abusing their power and their entire administration always covering up their mistakes! Why can't the rest of the world understand that we are all "Human Beings" and not different kind of people?

Why can't people stop being greedy and only look after themselves? Why can't we try to be better human beings and why do people ignore all the evilness the powerful people do? When will people rise up and not be afraid to say what is right and what is wrong? Well, if this is my purpose than I am not afraid anymore. I will tell the world the truth! The truth is that we are all "Human Beings" so stop being greedy and stop killing each other. If someone is trying to harm us than we have the right to protect ourselves, but when there is a group of human beings in a certain area, we shouldn't try to ruin their lives by arresting them, by harassing them, or by killing them for no reason. We are all human beings and we should all deserve a chance to live! Thank you mom for convincing God to have Alex come visit me because I know God doesn't try to do much to get involved in people's lives. I love you mom and I really hope I get to see you one day. I really hope we can talk so you can tell me about your life. I never got to talk to you and it hurts me every day that I never knew who you were. I really wish we can talk about the things I have done and the things you might not think would be ok. I LOVE you and I really hope we can meet one day.

Alex

What's up bro, this is really weird... I never thought in my life that I would see you get murdered in front of my eyes. I blame 100% myself because I would have jumped on top of you when the police were shooting at you because I didn't think they were shooting their real guns on you. I honestly thought they were shooting bean bags or rubber bullets because why aren't cops trained to be cops and not be criminals?

Remember that day when we got shot at by that Nazi when we left church that night. It was Epi, you, Peter, Juan, and me. Then when that guy almost hit Juan with his car, "Juan said, "Watch where you are driving!" And then that guy stopped and pealed out backwards and started shooting at us. I was behind everyone and started running so fast that I passed everyone and entered the store and jumped behind the counter. We always argued that I ran faster than you and I entered the store before you because you always said, " I (Alex) entered before everyone got to the store. But now you can have God to show you that night and show you that I entered the store first. Remember when I jumped behind the counter then you jumped behind the counter too and then you jumped on top of me so I didn't get shot. I still remember that day like it was yesterday. That Nazi had a machine gun and shot at us and all of us made it inside the store without dying. Remember that old guy who was working at the store that night? Remember, when he called the police to come and protect us, but when he told the police that a Nazi almost killed a lot of Mexicans, "The Police decided they didn't care so they didn't come to protect us." Remember, that old guy was like 60 years old and he called his friend to bring a gun. It was a revolver with only six bullets and he walked us back to the church. He had a cane and walked really slow. It was a little funny, but mainly scary walking back to the church because it was really dark and I kept on whispering, "He only has six bullets and that Nazi has a machine gun."

Remember, when we finally got back to the church and told our family what happened. Remember, I was in complete shock and I didn't realize I was shot in the leg until we were inside the church's bathroom. We stayed up all night praying and then the next day when it was sunny we left. Remember, that we saw the Nazi's car in the woods and it was all burnt up. The Nazi burnt up the car so he wouldn't be caught and the police were investigating the car. So please ask God to show you that night and he will show you that I was the person who ran the fastest and made it inside that store first. This is one of the reasons why I was so fast as a kid....... Because ever since that night, I used that night to make me run faster. That is how I became the fastest runner in my school even though you would always train me to run. Every time I was in a race or playing a sport, I would imagine that night and it would motivate me to run faster.

Remember all the things you taught me growing up? Remember all the games you came to see me play and remember all the people who were mad at me because I was so good at playing sports. Remember, when we went to Cost Cutter one night and the cashier said, "You are number 35 in basketball." And I said, "Yeah that is me." Well, my son played against you the other night and I kept on yelling, stop number 35!" And we both laughed and she asked, "How did you become so good?" And I said, "Well my brother right here taught me everything I know." And I saw you smile and you were so proud of me because you created a gifted kid who was superior in sports and you created a kid who was a genius in school and in life. You are the reason why I became a millionaire and you are the reason why I helped so many people.

Remember the last basketball game we played? You beat me and you know how much I hate losing so I want a rematch. Remember we never got to celebrate Christmas or birthdays because we didn't have the money. Well for my 10th birthday you surprised me because you worked for an entire month mowing laws and pulling out weeds from people's houses in order to buy a cake and a present for me. You bought me a telephone that was shaped of a basketball for my present. I remember how much that meant to me because you were always taking care of me. You were doing whatever it took to give me things so I could be happy. I love you bro.

Remember, the first time I won a poker tournament on-line? I made over $150,000 dollars! We put $20,000 in the bank so we could start saving money to give to your daughter when she turned 18 years old. (My brother Alex wanted to save money to give to her daughter when she turned 18 years old. When she turned 18 years old, my brother wanted to get back involved in her life, he was going to give her a lot of money that he saved up, and that is another reason why he stopped doing drugs and drinking alcohol. He wanted to prove to her that he was a good person again.) Since I won over $150,000 dollars, we decided to go to Las Vegas. We had a blast and we ended up spending $80,000 dollars. (The thing about my brother, even though he would be ok some days, well some days, he would just want to spend any money that he had on him so we spent $80,000 on a lot of stuff.)

You are the reason why I am an organ donor and I know you are an organ donor. After you were murdered, you couldn't even give your organs because these corrupted cops shot too many bullets into you. Again, I am sorry that I didn't jump on top of you.

Remember, when you taught me that if I ever became rich to not tell anyone? Well, I did become rich playing poker on-line and I never told anyone until I wrote this book. Remember, you told me to tell the truth on who I really am not too long ago, well that is what I am doing now. (Maybe God already told you what I was going to do?) Remember our plan, I was going to buy that store right next to my dad's house and we were going to both manage the business. Remember, I told you I had a friend who would invest in the business, well that person was me because I had the money to create a business with the money I won playing poker on-line. I was also going to help you out when your daughter turned 18 years old, she would see you are a good person who is doing good in life. I also set up an account with $200,000 dollars so you can go on a vacation with her, so you can buy a brand new car for her, so you can pay for her to go to college, so you can take her on a shopping spree, and so you can show her that you are a good person again. But I am so sorry that you can't do that anymore because I should have driven you to the hospital! I am so sorry that these cops don't know how to do their job and that is why I had to give up my soul so I can make it up to you. Please forgive me Alex, please tell mom that I am sorry that I might not be able to see her. Please tell God that I should have stopped gambling and I should have just used the money I had to start the business. I didn't want to start the business until another year because even though I had the money, I needed a little more, but now I realized that I was being greedy. So I am so sorry, but I am going to help your daughter so much so she can go to Heaven and you can see her again.

I have so much anger inside of me Alex! I don't know what to do and I don't know where to go? How am I suppose to get married? You were suppose to be my best man and now I can't even think about getting married in my future. I can't imagine doing anything in my life because what's the point? A cop can kill me tomorrow and try to cover it up again. Just like when they use to beat up African Americans and when they use to lynch them. I just don't understand why they can't put video cameras on Police Officers so people can see the TRUTH?

I know that things change in life and mostly everything happens for a reason. I don't know how much you can see me from Heaven so I am writing this book so you can read on what I am doing in my life. I am going to give your daughter any money the cops give us for your murder. I am also going to tell her what you told me when you were on the ground dying. I haven't told anyone what you told me because it is not there business. I cried so much because I didn't want you to die, but you knew you were dying so you whispered on what you wanted me to hear. However, that is when the cop tackled me off you and I still don't understand why the cop tackled me off you when I was giving you CPR and you were trying to talk to me. (I am not going to tell anyone what my brother told me that day because once his daughter is old enough, I will tell her what my brother's last words were.)

I have learned so much in my life that most people couldn't ever dream of learning. There is one thing that I have learned that I can't over come and that is if I want to move on with my life, then I must be able to rise above my past. Everything that I have done in my life, I have been proud of accomplishing. However, there is one thing that I am most proud of having and that is having the privilege of having you as my brother.

I have met a lot of people in my life that has influenced me to rise up and be something spectacular. However, putting all my feelings that I have toward my family and the people that I know, they do not come one tenth of how much I respect you, trust you, and love you. I have never said "Thank You" for everything that you did for me and I really wished I did so from the bottom of my heart.... "Thank you Alex." If you didn't teach me everything that I learned growing up, I wouldn't have accomplished so much in my life and I would have never been a good person. I am a genius because of you. I am a millionaire because of you. I have written four other books because of you, even though you always wanted to read them, well I am pretty sure God will let you read my books in Heaven.

The other thing I wanted to tell you is..... I don't know if God will tell you or not, but I gave up my soul so you can be in Heaven with our mom. I know you didn't go to church every week, I know you didn't pray every day, I know you did a lot of bad things growing up after you got hit in the head with the baseball bat. But I did so many good things in my life because of you and I am sacrificing my soul so you can be in Heaven and so God can give you one more chance in life and not be in Hell. I know you might not understand that I shouldn't have done that (Even though I am having tears writing this) But if I didn't have you in my life, I would have been a really bad person. So talk to God and tell God that our soul is one and if there is any way I can go to Heaven, I will do my best for the rest of my life to be a good person again. I know he must have sent you back to Earth for a few minutes to stop me from killing these cops for a reason. I am assuming there is a chance to make it to Heaven without my soul so I am going to do my best to do good things in life again. Tell my mom that I miss her and that even though I have done bad things from time to time, I am trying my best to help other people out again because I want to see her and talk to her.

On February 28th 2012, the day of your protest…. I did a press conference to honor who you were and told the truth about how the cops covered up your murder. The cops were still lying about your case so …. I opened up a suitcase with $ 1,000,000 dollars and said, "My dad and I are not lying! You cops murdered my brother and the rest of you cops helped them cover it up, but since you covered it up, there will not be any justice for my brother, but I am willing to give you $ 1,000,000 dollars to take a lie detector test so we can prove to the world that you covered up my brother's murder! And do you want to know what all the cops said………………, "No."

First everyone was shocked I had a million dollars and then everyone was shocked that the police said, "No." If they didn't lie or if they didn't cover up your murder then they would have take the lie detector test for one million dollars. My dad and I took the lie detector test twice and passed it twice. So Alex, I showed the world that they were the liars, the cowards, and the real criminals. I love you bro.

Am I in Hell?

"Where am I? This isn't real! I seriously thought I was in HELL and some times I still think I am in HELL. I keep telling myself the following:

This has to be hell because the cops are lying about everything on what they did to my brother!

This has to be hell because what kind of cops shoots a human being when they are on the ground?

This has to be hell because what kind of cop tackles a human being giving another human being CPR!

This has to be hell because what kind of cops almost kills a human being for having a cell phone in their hand!

This has to be hell because I have done so many good things in life and I saw my brother get executed in front of my eyes!

This has to be hell because everyone is going back to work after the funeral!

This has to be hell because a lot of people went on vacation after the funeral!

This has to be hell because a lot of people weren't feeling my pain!

This has to be hell because my brother isn't here anymore!

This has to be hell because my dad is crying every day!

This has to be hell because none of my family members want to kill these cops!

This has to be hell because I get really bad migraines and the pain isn't going away!

This has to be hell because why doesn't my brother want me to hurt these people? Is the Devil messing with my mind?

This has to be hell because every day cops are abusing their power and nothing is being done to stop it!

This has to be hell because every day I have to stop demons from entering and controlling my mind!

This has to be hell because I have to convince myself every day not to kill myself!

This has to be hell because I don't know what to do?

This has to be hell because Alex will not be my best man if I ever get married!

This has to be hell because no matter how much money I have or don't have, Alex isn't coming back!

This has to be hell because I don't know who I am anymore!

This has to be hell because I have been thinking so many evil things after my brother was murdered!

This has to be hell because I think in five or ten years people are going to come up to me and say, "Yeah, this is Hell and we have been fucking with your head." Ha Ha Ha, you stupid piece of worthless human being....?

This has to be hell because I am paying someone so I can beat him up with punching gloves and then I am paying another person to beat me up with punching gloves so the evilness can get out of me and to get the pain out of me!

This has to be hell because I have to handcuff myself some nights so I don't harm these cops!

This has to be hell because I know someone will be

NEXT!

How do I know if this isn't HELL? To be 100% honest with everyone again, two days after the funeral, I went back home. When I was home, I grabbed my video camera and my gun that I bought. I said the following, "This can't be real! Why the fuck is this happening? So this has to be Hell! I need to wake up and get out of this horrible nightmare! To my Sister and to my Dad, I am sorry, but Alex was too important in my life and I failed him. I told him everything would be ok and things didn't turn out Ok and I need to find him. So please forgive me one day and I really hope you understand why I had to do this.

To the cops who murdered my brother and to all the cops who keep on harassing minorities, to the cops who keep on abusing their power, and to the cops who kill innocent human beings, YOU WIN, I can not beat you? I always have walked away from your illegal tactics because no matter what I do, you won't stop being hateful people so congratulations, YOU win.

Then I got my gun and put it in my mouth, but I couldn't pull the trigger. Then I put the gun underneath my chin and I still couldn't pull the trigger. And finally, I put the gun right next to my ear and I could feel someone's was putting their hands on my shoulder? So I knew something or someone didn't want me to pull the trigger and that is when I decided to write this book to see what happens NEXT?

So am I in Hell or on Earth because these fucking corrupted cops murdered my brother and they are trying to cover up his murder! When will cops stop abusing their power? I keep telling myself that this isn't Hell, but it feels like it is hell. Is this Hell? This can't be Hell? Is this Hell? This can't be Hell? Wake up George. You need to wake up from this place! Is this Hell? This can't be Hell? Is this Hell? This can't be Hell? Wake up George. You need to wake up from this place! Is this Hell? This can't be Hell? Is this Hell? This can't be Hell? Wake up George. You need to wake up from this place!

I keep on telling myself these questions through out each day because I keep seeing my brother getting shot on the ground! I can't stop thinking on what happened on February 28th 2011! So I keep wondering if anything is real and wondering if those two cops really did shoot me?

Is this hell? This can't be Hell? Is this Hell? This can't be Hell? Wake up George. You need to wake up from this place! Is this Hell? This can't be Hell? Is this Hell? This can't be Hell? Wake up George. You need to wake up from this place! Is this Hell? This can't be Hell? Is this Hell? This can't be Hell? Wake up George. You need to wake up from this fucking nightmare!

My psychiatrist has given me all types of techniques to handle my anger, but they hardly ever work. She has given me different kind of medications, but they don't work. I pay her $400 dollars an hour and she is really smart. She has made me realize that these cops are lying because they are trying to survive. They don't want to go to jail for the rest of their lives and they know they screwed up so they will do anything to stay out of jail. Any criminal when he or she gets caught will do anything to survive. So now I understand why these cops are lying. I don't like why they are doing it, but at the same time I don't blame them as much anymore because I don't know what I would do if I accidently murdered some one by shooting them 13 times? However, it is really painful what I am going through.

Some days or nights I have so much pain inside me, I have to go outside and yell as hard as I can. I punch walls and start breaking things so my anger can get out of me. I do all this so I don't do something stupid and I am trying to be a good person again. Like I said before, I even have to handcuff myself to my bed on some nights. I know I am going to lose a lot of family member, friends, and I know a lot of people will not want to hang out with me or talk to me anymore. I understand that and respect their decisions. However, I need to find out the truth and find out who made the decision to cover up this murder. There has to be a guy in charge in the police administration that saw the facts and evidence and decided..... Shit, these guys really fucked up so we have to protect each other again! Do you know how to get away with murder? Become a cop!   I know a lot of people who looked at my headline of my book, expected to read "Cops murdered my brother so I should kill them!" The reason I did that was for marketing purposes. I knew if I had a good headline then more people would buy the book and hopefully try to make these cops wear video cameras so they can be protecting us and not killing us. But the truth is "Cops murdered my brother so what do I do now? I will fight for justice for all!"

How am I going to fight for justice for all? Well... I am not going to go after them to kill them, I am not going to be greedy like them, I am not going to pay people off people so people can believe my side of the story, I am not going to need anyone's help to believe in my faith, to believe in my destiny, and to believe in what I have to do in order to get justice.

I am not going to tell anyone my plan. I won't tell my dad, I won't tell my family members, I won't tell my pastor, I won't tell any of my friends, I won't tell any person who works for the law enforcement, and I won't tell any person who I see in this world. I will record a video message and put it in my bank vault because just incase these cops try to frame me for something stupid. Then I will have my lawyer from Las Vegas go into my bank vault and show the video of me in court and show what my ultimate plan was.

You have no clue what I am capable of doing

You have no clue how much pain I am in!

And you have no clue on what I am going to do because this is going to take years to set up and when the time does arrive....?

Cops Murdered my brother so what do I do now?

Medical examiner:

Even though I am a little upset with you, I am not going to go after you because you aren't worth my time and you gave a decent autopsy report.

Officer #1 Mr. Red:

You shot my brother seven times and you were the one who picked up the flashlight. You and officer #2 are probably not going to be convicted of murder so I am going to do my own justice. I am going to take my time learning how to torture someone without killing a person. Since my brother advised me that I shouldn't kill you, I am going to make sure you can't do this again. I am going to find out your working patterns, your social life patterns, and I am going to find the perfect time to meet you. When I do meet you then I am going to cut your trigger fingers. Since you might learn how to use your trigger fingers on your other hand than I am going to cut both hand's trigger fingers. Then I am going to cut your tongue and then put a chemical in one or two eyes depending on how much information you give me. If you give me the right information than I might let you keep both eyes, but most likely I will put a chemical in one of your eyes so you can be blind in one of them. The reason I am cutting your tongue and making you blind in one of your eyes is because you are lying about what you saw and lying on what you said. Even though I am going to torture you and make you disabled, I am still going to give you 100K in cash so you can try to live a life after this happens. I want you to be alive for the rest of your life so you can feel my brother's pain and so you can feel my pain. I am giving you the money because I know its going to be hard to have a job so use the money wisely after I torture you. Remember, I am a very wealthy person and I have great connections so be 100% honest with me when I ask you the following questions. I am already going to have the answers before I ask you the questions, but I am still going to ask you the questions to determine how much to torture you.

    1. Who's idea was it to tell everyone my brother had a hammer instead of the flashlight?

    2. Where is the flashlight that my brother had in his hand because the detective didn't have the flashlight so obviously someone took that flashlight and hid it somewhere?

    3. Did you or officer #2 put my brother finger's on the hammer in which you claim he had so his fingerprints were on it?

    4. Why did you tackle me off my brother when I was giving him CPR?

    5. Who's idea was it to fire the taser after my dad and I were taken out of the garage?

    6. Why did you drag my brother's body closer to the door?

    7. Why the fuck did you keep shooting my brother when he was on the ground?

    8. Who trained you to become a police officer?

    9. Are you sorry for what happened to my brother?

    10. How does it feel that I can snap my fingers and I can kill you any time that I want, but I chose not to because I am better then you?

11. How does it feel that the person you killed, is the same person who told me not to kill you because he knows we are going to walk you to the gate of Hell?

12. How does it feel that a Mexican has done more things than you can ever do in your life time? Don't you get it yet, I am not a Mexican, I am a human being just like you, so stop abusing your power and stop harassing and killing innocent people or you will go to that gate of Hell and trust me... You don't want to see that gate of Hell!

13. How does it feel that you killed a part of a human being, but not the entire human because Alex and I shared our lives together!

14. Don't you guys understand when you keep harassing or killing a certain type of people, you are killing more than just one good human being in this world? Don't you think there are "Real" consequences in this world and in the next world?

Officer #2 Mr. Orange:

You shot at my brother six times and you were the one who said, "I thought he had a hammer?" You and officer #1 are probably not going to be convicted of murder so I am going to do my own justice. I am going to take my time learning how to torture someone without killing a person. Since my brother advised me that I shouldn't kill you, I am going to make sure you can't do this again. I am going to find out your working patterns, your social life patterns, and I am going to find the perfect time to meet you. When I do meet you then I am going to cut your trigger fingers. Since you might learn how to use your trigger fingers on your other hand than I am going to cut both hand's trigger fingers. Then I am going to cut your tongue and then put a chemical in one or two eyes depending on how much information you give me. If you give me the right information than I might let you keep both eyes, but most likely I will put a chemical in one of your eyes so you can be blind in one of them. The reason I am cutting your tongue and making you blind in one of your eyes is because you are lying about what you saw and lying on what you said. Even though I am going to torture you and make you disabled, I am still going to give you 100K in cash so you can try to live a life after this happens. I want you to be alive for the rest of your life so you can feel my brother's pain and so you can feel my pain. I am giving you the money because I know its going to be hard to have a job so use the money wisely after I torture you. Remember, I am a very wealthy person and I have great connections so be 100% honest with me when I ask you the following questions. I am already going to have the answers before I ask you the questions, but I am still going to ask you the questions to determine how much to torture you.

1. Who's idea was it to tell everyone my brother had a hammer instead of the flashlight?

2. Where is the flashlight that my brother had in his hand because the detective didn't have the flashlight so obviously someone took that flashlight and hid it somewhere?

3. Did you or officer #1 put my brother finger's on the hammer in which you claim he had so his fingerprints were on it?

4. Why didn't you give my brother CPR when I kept on yelling at you guys that my brother was still trying to breathe?

5. Who's idea was it to fire the taser after my dad and I were taken out of the garage?

6. Why the fuck did you keep shooting my brother when he was on the ground?

7. Who trained you to become a police officer?

8. Are you sorry for what happened to my brother?

9. How does it feel that I can snap my fingers and I can kill you any time that I want, but I choose not to because I am better then you?

10. How does it feel that the person you killed, is the same person who told me not to kill you because he knows we are going to walk you to the gate of Hell?

11. How does it feel that I paid $40K to get all of your information, but someone at your job doesn't like you so he refused our money. So I used the 40K to help out a family in need.

12. How does it feel that a Mexican has done more things than you can ever do in your life time? Don't you get it yet, I am not a Mexican, I am a human being just like you, so stop abusing your power and stop harassing and killing innocent people or you will go to that gate of Hell and trust me... You don't want to see that gate of Hell!

13. How does it feel that you killed a part of a human being, but not the entire human because Alex and I shared our lives together!

14. Don't you guys understand when you keep harassing or killing a certain type of people, you are killing more than just one good human being in this world? Don't you think there are "Real" consequences in this world and in the next world?

Officer #3 Mr. Yellow:

You were the officer who was grabbed my brother when he was falling down. Remember, I am a very wealthy person and I have great connections so be 100% honest with me when I ask you the following questions. I am already going to have the answers before I ask you the questions, but I am still going to ask you the questions to determine how much to torture you.

1. Who's idea was it to say my brother had a hammer and why did you go along with the lie?

2. You kept on saying, "I am ok, I am ok." When you were on the ground, so why did you change your story that you were severely hurt?

3. Did anyone offer you a career advancement or money to keep the lie continue?

4. I kept on yelling at you to give my brother CPR, why didn't you help him?

5. Are you sorry for what happened to my brother?

6. How does it feel that a Mexican has done more things than you can ever do in your life time? Don't you get it yet, I am not a Mexican, I am a human being just like you, so stop abusing your power and stop harassing and killing innocent Human Beings!

Officer #4 Mr. White:

You were the cop who tried to stop me front entering the garage. Remember, I am a very wealthy person and I have great connections so be 100% honest with me when I ask you the following questions. I am already going to have the answers before I ask you the questions, but I am still going to ask you the questions to determine how much to torture you.

1. You were there so why didn't you tell your boss that you were there? (When the police report first came out, they said only three police officers were on scene, but you were there too!)

2. Did anyone offer you a career advancement or money to keep the lie continue?

3. Are you admitting the truth on what you saw or are the police keeping you quiet? Or are you going to find a way to say you weren't there?

4. I kept on yelling at you to give my brother CPR, why didn't you help him?

5. Are you sorry for what happened to my brother?

6. How does it feel that a Mexican has done more things than you can ever do in your life time? Don't you get it yet, I am not a Mexican, I am a human being just like you, so stop abusing your power and stop harassing and killing innocent Human Beings!

Officer #5 Mr. Black:

You were the cop who almost murdered me because you thought I had a gun, but I had a cell phone! Remember, I am a very wealthy person and I have great connections so be 100% honest with me when I ask you the following questions. I am already going to have the answers before I ask you the questions, but I am still going to ask you the questions to determine how much to torture you.

1. Are you blind because how do you think my cell phone was a gun?

2. Did anyone offer you a career advancement or

money to keep the lie continue?

3. Why did you search my dad and I for weapons after you almost murdered me!

4. If you would have shot and killed me, would you have placed a gun on me?

5. Why did you say, "Last warning?" (Do you know how much I think about those seconds before I jumped onto the ground?) Every fucking night I am wondering if you shot me and killed me and if I am in hell?

6. Are you sorry for what happened to my brother?

7. How does it feel that a Mexican has done more things than you can ever do in your life time? Don't you get it yet, I am not a Mexican, I am a human being just like you, so stop abusing your power and stop harassing and killing innocent Human Beings!

Officer #6 Mr. Purple:

You were the other officer that thought I had a gun! Remember, I am a very wealthy person and I have great connections so be 100% honest with me when I ask you the following questions. I am already going to have the answers before I ask you the questions, but I am still going to ask you the questions to determine how much to torture you.

1. Are you blind because how do you think my cell phone was a gun?

2. Did anyone offer you a career advancement or money to keep the lie continue?

3. If you would have shot and killed me, would you have placed a gun on me?

4. Why did you search my dad and I for weapons after

you almost killed me!

5. Are you sorry for what happened to my brother?

6. How does it feel that a Mexican has done more things than you can ever do in your life time? Don't you get it yet, I am not a Mexican, I am a human being just like you, so stop abusing your power and stop harassing and killing innocent human beings!

Detective Blue:

Do you know why the detective told us from the beginning of the case why he wouldn't come to our house? The reason he didn't want to come to our house to get our side of the story was.... Because he and the police have already made their decision on how my brother was murdered. They took whatever evidence they had and made it seem like my brother had a hammer and was attacking the officer. So if he came to our house and if we showed him inch by inch on where everything was at and exactly what happened then he would have a really hard time to dispute on what we saw and where all the "Real" evidence was at. However, remember what he said, "It would be pointless to come to your house." I know the detective is going to read this and say, "Wait, why didn't you tell me everything?" Well, because I don't trust you. Ever since you decided to not come to our house, I knew you were trying to help out the other cops. If I would have told you everything I saw and everything that happened, you and your buddies would find a way to make my story not credible and have another theory to make it seem like I was lying.

Thank you Detective Blue, thank you very much on what I have to do to you and the people who are trying to cover this murder up. I was going to give you one more chance if you would have asked my dad's lawyer or me for a follow up question or another reason, but instead... You decided to close the case and go on your vacation. Thank you very much so what am I going to do to Detective Blue, well I am going to either cut all his toes from his feet. Or, depending on how much information he gives me about his "Investigation" then I might just cut five toes from his left or right foot. Remember, I am a very wealthy person and I have great connections so be 100% honest with me when I ask you the following questions. I am already going to have the answers before I ask you the questions, but I am still going to ask you the questions to determine how much to torture you.

1. Did you really think the officer was hit with a hammer?

2. What was the real reason why you didn't come to our house?

3. How many different stories did the officers tell you on what happened?

4. Did anyone promise you a career advancement or money to believe the cops lies?

5. So is this pointless to do? Remember, like you said, "It will be pointless to come to your house."

6. Are you sorry for what happened to my brother?

7. Which toes do you want me to cut, the left or right, or how about we cut both feet?

8. How does it feel that a Mexican has done more things than you can ever do in your life time? Don't you get it yet, I am not a Mexican, I am a human being just like you, so stop abusing your power and stop harassing and killing

innocent Human Beings!

9. How does it feel that I have written this book and you are probably going to get fired?

Sheriff who did the press conference:

First I am going to ruin your campaign. I know you are trying to get re-elected in 2011 for your job position so I am going to contribute money so you can't get your job. However, if by some miracle you get your job again, we will meet one night and I am going to cut your tongue. First, I am going to ask you some questions.

1. What information were you given before you made the press conference?

2. Did you really not know how many shots were fired?

3. Why did you keep on bringing up my brother's past history?

4. Didn't your people tell you that my dad and I were arguing with your officers that my brother had a flashlight?

5. Are you sorry for what happened to my brother?

6. How does it feel that a Mexican has done more things than you can ever do in your life time? Don't you get it yet, I am not a Mexican, I am a human being just like you, so stop abusing your power and stop harassing and killing innocent Human Beings!

Unit Supervisor from Crime Victim Program:

Even though I am very disappointed in you; You are a female and I don't hit or harm females. If you were a male, I would have cut off the ear you used to get your information from Detective Blue. However, since you are a female, I have no choice, but to not harm you.

After years of analyzing on how to torture someone and after years of monitoring the people who I am going after then I will go after Police Officer #1 and Police Officer #2 first. When I am done torturing them so they can feel my pain then I will have them handcuffed and I will drop them off at the emergency room so they can get medical help. I will take care of these two people the same day and then hopefully the rest of the people will go on television and apologize for their lies and corruption. If they don't then I will be in another country where the government can't go after me. Then after a few years waiting, I will come back and do the same thing to Officer # 3 and Officer #4. I will hope the rest of the people go on television and apologize for their lies and corruption. If they don't then I will be in another country again where the government can't go after me. Then after a few years waiting, then I will go after Officer #5 and Officer #6. I will hope the rest of the people go on television and apologize for their lies and corruption. If they don't then I will be in another country again where the government can't go after me. Then after a few years waiting, then I will go after the detective and the other person who didn't want to put these cops in jail.

I know you are probably wondering how I will find these people because they will probably move after these events happen. However, it's pretty easy to find someone with the right connections and the right amount of money. All I want is my mind back to be some what "Normal" again. They took that away from me when they went on television with their lies and their cover up. Well, enough is enough so all they have to do is go back on television and admit they screwed up and lied. However, I really doubt they will go on television and admit the truth. So that is why I have to do what I have to do.

What is worst? A person who is criminal all his life or a person who is a good person, a millionaire, and a genius, but when the police brutally murder his brother in front of his eyes and call him a liar and a criminal and that person can go after these corrupted cops and make them feel his pain, what is worst?

To be 100% honest with everyone who reads this, if I shot someone because I thought he had a gun or hammer then I might have tried to cover it up too. But after praying for a long time, I would admit my mistake. Obviously these cops screwed up big time and to be 100% honest with you again, I don't want these cops to go to jail. I know my family and friends are going to hate me saying this, but I know these cops won't be found guilty for their crimes. I rather do my own justice because at best these cops are going to get 1-5 years in jail. However, if I do my own justice, these cops won't have a tongue and they will be blind in one of their eyes. Also they won't have their trigger fingers anymore so they will be disabled for the rest of their lives. So I think if I do my own justice then it would make their lives even worst instead of serving 1-5 years in jail. Then I know they will feel my pain for the rest of their lives, just like the pain that I feel every day waking up in the messed up world.

I didn't put these cop's names in my book because I don't want a person to harm these people. This is my situation and I will be the "person" who seeks justice. I don't want anyone to do something stupid and think they should do something. This is my purpose in life now and I will take care of it. Even if I go to Jail for the rest of my life and these cops are not in jail.... I know Alex and I will meet them in the after life and we will walk them to the GATE OF HELL and they will be begging us to not go to the GATE OF HELL, but I will say, "My brother and I gave you every day until the day you died to do the right thing, but you never did so now you must be punished. Even though I said some evil things again, I just wanted you to know the evil things I have been thinking, but I physically won't harm them.

So why did I write this book? Every time people ask me, "What are you going to do in life now since your brother was murdered?" Well, I am tired of being arrested and I am tired of cops not being trained to do their job. Either cops are not properly trained or these cops are being trained to arrest and kill minorities! Also I need to make myself good again by seeing a psychiatrist, pray every day, go to church, talk to my pastor as much as possible, and do whatever it takes to be a good person again and not be a evil person. Every time I tell what happens to my brother, everyone says, "I am sorry." Well, to the people who are sorry, all I ask is that you write to the congress and say the following:

Dear Congress,

Who is next?

There are hundreds of thousands of people who get arrested every year or harassed every year for no reason. Cops are always using different "tatics" to try to make an arrest. There are so many innocent and good people who are getting tired of cops who are not trained properly. When will you train cops to do their job better? I know there are a lot of good cops, but year after year so many people get handcuffed without being reported. There are so many cops who think they have so much power and they abuse their power. We believe with the technology of today, cops should have video cameras on them when they are doing their jobs.

Every cell phone has a video camera and so many other technologies have video cameras, why can't police have a little video camera on them so when they do their job, we all know they are doing it right. I know it wouldn't cost that much to put a little video camera onto a uniform of a police officer so please use our tax money to train cops better and to put video cameras on them so we know, we can trust them. If someone murders a cop, that person gets the death penalty so lets show the world that police officers are good people that are trying to protect us. We don't want these video cameras on Police Officers in a couple years, we don't want them next year, we don't want them in a month, we don't want them tomorrow, we need these video cameras on Police Officers today so we can save lives! And prove us wrong that cops don't abuse their power!

1. Having a little video camera on a police officer will not cost much.

2. Our tax money pay for police officers salaries so they work for us and we don't work for them.

3. When a crime does happen, the people can see in court what the police officer saw the day of the crime.

4. Police officers can be more efficient with their jobs by seeing their tactics or mistakes on video.

5. Police will not harass, abuse their power, or beat up people as much anymore because they are being monitored.

6. Police won't be able to take bribes on the job.

7. You can save lives by putting a video camera on police officers!

8. You can monitor what cops are doing at the police station and when a police officer needs help and can't call for help, you would be able to get that police officer help sooner!

9. Do you want your kid to be harassed or arrested like my family, friends, and I have been because we are minorities?

10. You are being greedy and you are abusing your power so do you want to go to the gate of Hell? Why do cops have to abuse their power?

Our taxes pay for them to protect us! They are not getting paid to be racist, to be harassing people, to be abusing their power, and to get away with murder! Do you know when we catch police officers beating up a person on a someone's video camera, the police always go on television and say, "We are going to do a full investigation." Why the fuck do you need to use our tax money to do an investigation? If I work in a bank or work at Mc Donald's and beat up a customer for no reason, my boss wouldn't do an investigation, he would fire me that same day he saw me beat up a customer on the video camera! Are you still wondering why I don't pay all my taxes?

Who is next?

Do you know why the number one reason I haven't had a kid yet? Well, because I don't want my kid to enter a world where the cops abuse their power and try to make minorities feel like they are not human beings!

To all the readers, imagine yourself 50 years from now. Will the minorities still be the minorities? Imagine the day when the Caucasian will become the minority? My brother and I believe every person is a human being and should be treated equal. However, when the Caucasian people become the minority, wouldn't they want to be treated equal and not be harassed every time they get pulled over? Or harassed when there is a burglary? Or harassed when a murder happens? I really hope we can rise above our past problems and can say, "We are better than that and we want everyone to be treated equal and to be treated like a human being." I know a lot of people are saying, "Well this doesn't happen because we have a African American president now." Do you think cops are going to stop doing what they are doing since we have a minority president or do you think they will do more crimes because of that reason? I am not asking people to harm another human being, I am not asking for the police to go to jail, I am not asking for money........ I am only asking for enough votes so we can put video cameras on police officers so we can save lives! This is my ultimate goal in life now, to save lives by having police to have video cameras on them.

So congratulations cops..... You finally did it, you made a good person become a very bad person. However, you can make a good person be good again by doing the right thing, by telling the truth or by putting a video camera on a police officer. Once we have video cameras on a Police Officer, then I will know I am back on Earth and people are trying to help people and trying to save lives.

Even though I have said I want to hurt these people....Well, I am not going to do anything to hurt them physically. I just have evil thoughts after I saw my brother get brutally murdered. I know I won't hurt them, but I just wanted the cops to read on how bad I have been thinking every day. I am just going to tell the truth and continue to help people in this world so one day I can see my mom and my brother again because "Cops murdered my brother so now I am going to fight for justice!" I really hope we get enough votes so cops can have video cameras on their uniforms, but I can only hope for the best.

Even though I won't hurt these cops
I will cut my middle finger and give it to the police stations
That murdered my brother

"Cops murdered my brother so what do I do now?"

Dear Reader,

Do you know how hard it is for me to try to live a good life again? Do you know how hard it was to write this book? I cried for hours every time I had to try to write this book. I have to carry my handcuffs every where I go. Either it's in my car or at home. Isn't it ironic that I was always getting hand cuffed by cops because they were abusing their power, but now I am hand cuffing myself to not harm them? I am seeing my psychiatrist three times a week for two hours a day. I am praying for most of the day and going to church as much as possible. I am talking to my pastor everyday and I am trying my hardest to be a good person again, but it has been really hard! Even though it's been really hard, I am slowly getting better.

I know a lot of readers are thinking, "Well since this is a fictional book than everything you say can all be lies." You are 100% right, but that is why if we get enough votes to put a video camera on a police officer, then you would be able to see what I saw and then I would have never written this book. The cover of this book is me.... I am wearing Alex's favorite hat, his shirt, his pants, and his shoes. The wood floor is where Alex was lying on the ground and where he was being shot and you will notice that the police took most of the wood apart to find bullets or bullet shells on the ground. If you look very closely, you can see one of the bullets hit the side of the house. After I saw my brother get brutally murdered, I am having a really hard time believing "If this world is Hell or Earth?" Why can't people stop being racist, stop being greedy, and why can't we try to help each other out?

1. Remember, the cops changed their story twice!

2. Remember, they said there was only three officers on scene, but there was four officers. (The fourth officer didn't want to go along with the other three officer's story.)

3. Remember, my brother was shot at 13 times and they took 10 bullets out of his body. (They were only three to five feet from my brother's body.)

4. Remember, the officers kept on shooting my brother on the ground after the first shot!

5. Remember, my brother didn't have any combative or defensive injuries. (If he was attacking an officer or if he knew he was going to get shot, he would have some marks claiming the officer's story.)

6. Remember, my brother didn't have any alcohol or any type of drugs in his body.

7. Remember, my dad called the police to find my brother and to take him to the hospital.

8. Remember, a border patrol agent came to the house and he was the first person who started shooting at my brother. (Why did the border patrol come to the house? We don't smuggle drugs or smuggle people, so they should have never went to my dad's house.)

9. Remember, the detective never wanted to go to my dad's house to get our side of the story. (The detective and the police have already concluded on what they wanted to say what happened at the house and they didn't want to know the truth!)

10. Remember, Officer #1 thought he heard a gun shot and Officer #2 thought they he saw a hammer.)

11. Remember, people will always believe a cop's side of the story and not what other people saw at the crime

scene.

12. Remember, they tackled me off my brother when I was giving him CPR and then they rolled my brother over onto his stomach while he was still alive to put handcuffs on him!

13. Remember, when I was going to dial 911 again to ask for help, Officer #5 and Officer #6 thought my cell phone was a gun! (Hopefully you the reader understand, cops do have a tough job to do, but they always think negative when they go to a house and figure a human being has a gun or some type of weapon in his hands!)

14. Remember, Officer #3 was released from the hospital within 24 hours.

15. Remember, they figured I was some poor uneducated Mexican who can't fight for justice. (However, I am a human being who has more knowledge than they could ever imagine!)

16. Remember, I don't want anyone to harm these police officers or any other police officer. (I just don't want this to happen to anyone else again.)

17. Remember, they think I will have a protest and they will only have one bad day of press. (However, they have no clue who I am and what I can do! I won't harm them physically, but I will do whatever it takes so this won't happen again!)

18. Remember, I am not selling this book for money, I am selling it to get enough votes to put video cameras on police officers uniform.

So please vote to get video cameras on police officer's uniforms. Trust me, it will stop cops harassing us, it will stop cops abusing their powers, and it will stop cops killing innocent human beings. And most importantly, you won't go through the pain on what I am going through every second of my life...

I was born with a heart like you.

I was born with a brain like you.

I was born with two eyes like you.

I was born with a liver like you.

I was born with two arms like you.

I was born with two legs like you.

I was born with veins like you.

I was born with two ears like you.

I was born with a soul like you.

And I bleed red just like you!

So when my brother told me when I was a baby, I am a human being......

Was he lying or

Are we all alike and really human beings?

To honor my brother on what he taught me:

"We are all created equal and there is only one race in this world and that is the "Human race."

Alejandro Perez Martinez